Stories from Panchatantra

Inspiring Immortal Tales through the Ages

Stories Retold by

Mahesh Chandra Bhargava

I10638326

PUSTAK MAHAL®
Delhi | Bangalore | Mumbai
Patna | Hyderabad

Publishers
Pustak Mahal®, Delhi

J-3/16 , Daryaganj, New Delhi-110002
☎ 23276539, 23272783, 23272784 • *Fax:* 011-23260518
E-mail: info@pustakmahal.com • *Website:* www.pustakmahal.com

London Office
5, Roddell Court, Bath Road, Slough SL3 OQJ, England
E-mail: pustakmahaluk@pustakmahal.com

Sales Centre
10-B, Netaji Subhash Marg, Daryaganj, New Delhi-110002
☎ 23268292, 23268293, 23279900 • *Fax:* 011-23280567
E-mail: rapidexdelhi@indiatimes.com

Branch Offices
Bangalore: ☎ 22234025
E-mail: pmblr@sancharnet.in • pustak@sancharnet.in
Mumbai: ☎ 22010941
E-mail: rapidex@bom5.vsnl.net.in
Patna: ☎ 3294193 • *Telefax:* 0612-2302719
E-mail: rapidexptn@rediffmail.com
Hyderabad: *Telefax:* 040-24737290
E-mail: pustakmahalhyd@yahoo.co.in

© **Pustak Mahal, Delhi**

ISBN 81-223-0454-0

Edition : January 2007

Printed at : Unique Colour Carton, Mayapuri, Delhi-110064

Contents

Part-II

MITRASAMPRAPTI

Part-III

KAKOLUKIYAM

Part-IV

LABDHAPRANASH

Part-V

APARIKSHIT KARAK

The Origin of Panchatantra

It is said that, in ancient times, there was a kingdom called 'Mahilaropya' in the southern part of India. The ruler, Amarshakti, was learned and pious and a real protector of his subjects. The people were happy and satisfied as there were allround prosperity, peace and good governance. The ruler was worried only on one count. His three sons, Bahushakti, Ugrashakti and Anantshakti were devoid of all that the princes should have. They paid no attention to their education and were extremely impolite and arrogant and were simpletons. They took no interest in matters relating to statecraft or religion.

One day, Amarshakti called his ministers and told them his problem. He said, "I am greatly worried about the illiteracy and behaviour of my sons. How would they run this kingdom after me? If a ruler is foolish and arrogant the kingdom is bound to disintegrate. The people will suffer and the whole society will go to dogs. A foolish and ill behaved person is like a barren woman or land which is of no use. Can you suggest ways by which my sons could become educated, wise and competent?"

His councillors gave different advices regarding educating the princes. One of them named Sumati advised the ruler to hand over the princes to the care of the renowned teacher Acharya Vishnu Sharma who might succeed in making the princes worldly-wise and informed in all matters of state.

The ruler turned to the venerable teacher and said that if he was successful in educating his sons, he would award him hundred villages. Vishnu Sharma smiled and said, "My king, I am now aged eighty years. I have seen and enjoyed everything that life can offer. I have no desires for worldly wealth. Besides, I believe that learning sold loses its lustre. I will teach and instruct the princes in all the arts and sciences within six months." The ruler apologised for offering him a reward and said, "You are the real teacher. As the Sun casts its rays on all without distinction, a really learned man spreads learning without any desire for reward or compensation."

The three princes were handed over to the Acharya. Vishnu Sharma started teaching them through the medium of stories that were instructive and full of worldly wisdom. He divided the stories in five parts—*Mitrabhed, Mitrasamprapti, Kakolukiyam, Labdhapranash* and *Aparikshit Karak.* That is why it came to be known as *Panchatantra.* Within six months the princes were changed persons as they became learned, worldly-wise and well versed in statecraft. It is said that anyone who imbibes the teachings of this book of wisdom can face all problems and situations in life with confidence.

❑ ❑ ❑

Part-I

MITRABHED

One should develop the capacity to differentiate between real friends and flatterers. Placing your trust in people who are not sincere may eventually prove disastrous as the world is full of people who will go any length to serve their own interests.

1. Never Seek Advice from an Enemy

Many families of storks had made their homes on a huge banyan tree in a forest. A deadly cobra also lived in the hollow of that tree. Whenever the cobra got an opportunity, it came out of the hole and ate the fledglings. The storks were miserable but did not know what to do to stop the killing of their offsprings. Their chief, one day sat near a pond shedding tears when a crab passed by. The crab was happy to see his natural enemy in that miserable state. He extended fake sympathy and asked the reason for the stork's distress.

The stork related the tale of his misery. The crab thought that it was a good opportunity to settle scores with his natural enemies. He said, "Uncle, the solution of your problem is simple. Spread fish meat from the burrow of a mongoose to the hollow of the tree where the cobra lives. The mongoose will come eating the meat and finding a snake, will kill it."

The stork liked the idea and left a trail of dead fish from the burrow of the mongoose to the tree. The mongoose saw it and came eating the fish. As he reached the hollow of the tree, he found the cobra coiled inside pounced on it and killed it.

As he looked around, he saw a lot of storks living there and started killing them one by one till the entire flock was liquidated. This story tells us that never be friends or take advice from your enemy.

❏ ❏ ❏

2. The Story of Sanjivak and Pingalak

A businessman named Vardhman lived in the city of Mahilaropya in the southern region. He had earned a lot of money but still desired to earn more. He decided to go to Mathura for this purpose. He told his wife of his plans. She opposed it saying, "You have plenty of money and wealth. I see no wisdom in counting unforeseen troubles in a foreign place." Vardhman countered her argument and said, "In this world, money is all powerful. If you do not go on adding to your assets, they may be depleted. The common people look upon a moneyed man as wise and learned. Nothing is unattainable for a wealthy person. A poor man commands no respect in society. Even parents do not bother about a poor son."

Vardhman decided on the items he would deal in at Mathura. They were loaded on bullock carts. His favourite bullocks—Sanjivak and Nandan—were yoked to his personal cart. He loved these bulls as his sons as they were born in his house. After making all arrangements, this caravan of bullock carts started on its journey to Mathura which was, at that time, a renowned centre of trade and commerce.

After travelling for many days, Vardhman's caravan reached the outskirts of Mathura. Unfortunately his cart got stuck in the marshy land on the bank of river Yamuna. The bullocks tried their best to pull out the cart but could not. In the efforts, Sanjivak broke his leg. Vardhman tried his best to free and bring out his favourite bullock but failed. He kept on trying for three days but

Sanjivak could not be brought out. The servants were getting restive. They told Vardhman that there was danger of their falling prey to dacoits or wild animals if they stayed longer at that place. Eventually they prevailed on Vardhman to leave Sanjivak to his fate and proceed to Mathura. Vardhman reluctantly agreed to their suggestion and left two men to look after Sanjivak. They both abandoned Sanjivak and joined their master at Mathura. They concocted a story that the bull died of his injuries and they cremated him on the spot. Vardhman grieved for Sanjivak but accepted it as the will of God.

Sanjivak was sad at being left to his fate like that. He thought to himself, "It is true that, in times of adversity, even your own shadow abandons you. I have served my master loyally all these years and when I needed his support he abandoned me. In this world you become dispensable if you have no utility value." He decided to make all efforts to free himself. At first, he did not succeed but eventually was able to come out of the swamp. It did not take him long to regain his strength as he had full run of the place. He grazed on the soft and green grass of the river bank and soon became very strong, so much so that when he bellowed, it echoed in the entire forest and could frighten the bravest.

One day, Pingalak, a lion came to the river bank to quench his thirst with his attendants. As he heard the roar of Sanjivak, he thought that some very powerful animal was living on the river bank. He got so frightened that he left the place with his courtiers and even thought of leaving that forest for safety. Two jackals named Karkat and Damanak, who had sometime back worked as ministers of the lion Pingalak, saw all this from a distance. They had been dismissed for corruption but still followed Pingalak in the hope of getting restored to their former position. They started talking to each other about what they had seen.

13

Damanak said, "Our king seems to be scared of something."

"How can you say that?" his brother Karkat querried.

"Did you not see him running away without drinking at the river? It was quite evident from his face and eyes. We must find out the reason," Damanak said.

Karkat advised him not to poke his nose in something that did not concern him. He might get into trouble. Damanak was adamant. He thought that it may provide them both an opportunity to retrieve their lost status. He decided to investigate the cause of Pingalak's behaviour. Damanak approached Pingalak and greeted him. Pingalak said, "How are you Damanak? Seeing you after a long time." "Sir, I am still your loyal servant. Your welfare is uppermost in my mind. Just now, I have come to talk about something that I would like to discuss with you in private." Everybody left as Pingalak gestured.

Damanak got closer as everyone left. "Your majesty seems to be worried about something. If you confide in me, may be I can help you. Believe me, I will not hesitate to even lay down my life for you." Pingalak told him his fears about some ferocious animal living in that forest and that he was thinking of migrating elsewhere.

Damanak immediately guessed that Pingalak was terrified. He said, "My lord, one should not give up one's rights without fighting for them. It does not behove a king to run away like this. If you so desire I can find out who that animal is that has scared you to this extent.

Pingalak was duly impressed and asked him to investigate. He also assured Damanak that he still had great affection for him. Bidding goodbye Damanak left for the swamp of Yamuna. He hid himself behind a thick bush to have a look at the animal that had frightened Pingalak. Soon he espied Sanjivak roaming about. For the other wild animals of the forest a bullock may be a strange thing, but Damanak had seen many of these grass eating domestic animals in villages. He thought it prudent not to disclose the identity of the animal to Pingalak so he remained scared of him.

He returned to Pingalak and informed him that not only did he see the ferocious animal but he even talked to that ferocious animal that was stalking the river bank. He further told that the powerful animal was under protection of God Shankar himself. Pingalak felt the ground slipping from under his feet as he heard this. But Damanak assured him, "You need not fear him. Though I am a weak person, my lord, I am gifted with an excellent brain. If you desire I can produce him before you."

"If you do that, I shall restore you to a prime position amongst my ministers," Pingalak gratefully assured him. Damanak, a wily person, told him that he had no need for an official position. He was doing it, he said, as it was his duty to serve him as a loyal subject.

Damanak found Sanjivak lying in the sun contentedly chewing the cud. He boldly approached him and said, "You good for nothing bull, how dare you disturb the peace of the forest? Our king Pingalak is furious and has called you." Sanjivak enquired about the identity of Pingalak. He was completely unnerved when told that Pingalak the lion was the ruler of that forest. He asked Damanak to intercede on his behalf and get him pardoned. Damanak pretended that it was not an easy task but as he seemed to be a gentle person, he would try his best. He asked Sanjivak to follow him. As they reached the edge of the forest, he advised the bull to wait there so that he could go ahead and assuage the anger of Pingalak.

Then he went to Pingalak and informed him that Sanjivak is willing to come and be your friend if he is assured safety of his life. Pingalak was extremely pleased to hear this and asked Damanak to fetch the bull assuring him of his friendship and security of life. On hearing this Sanjivak felt relieved and grateful to Damanak and vowed eternal friendship with him. Damanak then took Sanjivak to the lion. Pingalak received him warmly and asked him to live fearlessly in the forest as he was not only an honoured guest but a brother.

Damanak was appointed prime minister while his brother Karkat became a minister. Karkat acknowledged his brother as a master diplomat who had so cleverly got back his authority and position. Damanak said it was nothing. Now he would take steps to consolidate his power and have the king eating from his hands.

The friendship between Pingalak and Sanjivak grew day by day. Sanjivak had a deep knowledge of religious and moral principles that he had imbibed by listening to the discourses of learned men at Vardhman's place. They spent most of their time together and soon the lion started neglecting his duties. Taking advantage of the situation, ministers and soldiers felt free to act in any manner they pleased. There was total anarchy in the kingdom. Karkat asked his brother to set things right.

Damanak asked him to be patient as he now intended to sow the seeds of discord between the lion and the bull and thus get rid of Sanjivak and further consolidate his position.

He went to Pingalak and informed him that he had some bad news for him. He informed him that Sanjivak planned to kill him and become king. Pingalak was shocked to hear this. He could not imagine that one whom he treated as his brother would turn a traitor. Damanak told him not to grieve over his friend's treachery as, in this world, even a brother would not hesitate to stab him in the back for kingdom, position and wealth. He would see to it that no harm came to him.

Damanak went straight to Sanjivak and informed him that Pingalak intended to kill him as he feared that he would one day dethrone him. As he was his friend he was forewarning him. Sanjivak regretted the day he agreed to be the lion's friend. He thought it was foolish of him to trust a wild and natural enemy. Water and fire can never co-exist. For a while, he thought of running away but then decided to face the situation boldly.

Next day, when he went to the court of Pingalak, he found the lion in an angry mood looking at him with blood red eyes. Sanjivak also stared at him in an angry manner. Pingalak was convinced that Sanjivak wanted to kill him. He pounced on him and a fight ensued between them. Sanjivak fought bravely but eventually lay dead. Pingalak was also grievously injured. All the animals were also perplexed at the sudden turn of events. Karkat immediately guessed that it was all his brother's doing. He took Damanak aside and chastised him for making two friends fight each other. Damanak replied, "A diplomat never bothers about the means to gain his objectives. If one is to think of morality how could one improve one's status in life? The road to power is not paved with ideals and good conduct." Karkat was furious and replied that he did not want to associate with such a foolish king and unscrupulous brother and left the place.

On his part, Pingalak felt a tinge of remorse for killing his friend. He cast a last glance at Sanjivak's inert body and left to take some rest accompanied by wily Damanak.

❑ ❑ ❑

3. Look Before You Leap

A lion named Madotkat lived in some forest. A tiger, a jackal, a wolf, a crow and an owl were his attendants. They also depended on the lion for their food and other necessities. One day a camel lost his way and strayed into that forest. As soon as the jackal saw him he rushed to the lion and informed him about the intruder. The jackal said, "The newcomer does not seem to belong to any wild species." The lion called the owl and ordered him to investigate. After some time the owl returned and told the lion, "My lord, He is a camel. He is a domesticated animal and you have every right to kill him and make a feast of him."

The lion thought for a moment and said, "No, I cannot do it. He is our guest. Do you not know that it is a sin to kill even an enemy who takes refuge in you? Bring him here and tell him that he would be under our protection. I will enquire from him the reason of his coming into the forest."

The crow brought him before the lion assuring him that no harm would come to him. The camel told the lion, "My lord, my name is Kathnak. I got separated from my herd and have strayed into this forest." The lion replied, "It is alright. Now you need not go back to the village and cartloads. You can live here fearlessly. There is ample food for you in this forest."

From that day Kathnak became part of the lion's entourage. Being a herbivore, he did not face any shortage of food and soon gained weight. It so happened that a rogue elephant came into that forest. He started terrorising the inhabitants of the forest. The lion had to fight him to protect his subjects. They fought fiercely. The lion was able to kill him in the end. But the elephant grievously injured him with his sharp tusks. The lion became incapable of hunting, with the result that his attendants faced starvation.

Seeing their plight, the lion called them and told them to bring some wild animal whom he could kill easily so that all of them had some food. The attendants searched throughout the forest but could not find any prey. They started consultations amongst themselves. The jackal suggested, "Friends, there is no sense in wandering in search of food. Why not kill Kathnak? His body can provide food for days." The crow reminded him that the lion had promised him protection and would never agree to kill him to satisfy his hunger.

The jackal said, "Do not worry. I have a plan and our master will not object to kill him." Then he took them all into confidence and told them his plan. The jackal approached the lion and said, "Sir, we have searched throughout the forest but could not find any prey. I suggest that you kill Kathnak." The lion was beside himself with rage and roared, "You wicked jackal. You are asking me to commit such a sin. Can I kill one who is my guest and to whom I have promised protection? How could you suggest something so atrocious? Get out of my sight or I will kill you."

The jackal said, "My master, listen to me for a while. I agree it would be a sin to kill him, but, suppose, he himself offers to be killed due to his sense of loyalty for what you have done for him. There would be no harm in killing him." The lion was also feeling the pangs of hunger and hence agreed to kill the camel if he offered himself voluntarily.

They got together and went to the lion resting under a tree. First the crow approached him, "My master, we have been unable to find any food. I offer myself. Please kill me and satisfy your hunger. As it is, the servant who lays down his life for the master earns merit." The owl also came forward to do the same. The jackal came forward and said, "Both of you have very little flesh on your body. Our master will still be hungry. I offer my body to our master." Hearing this, the tiger came forward and said, "You also do not have much flesh on your body. After all you eat food that is rotten. It is written in religious books that one should not eat improper food even in the face of death due to starvation. You are animals with claws and as such are not proper food for the master. Please move aside and let me offer my body to our lord."

As the tiger came forward, the lion said, "You belong to the same species of the cat family. Can I kill someone of my own family. That would not be proper." Kathnak saw and heard all this. He thought to himself, "The lion has refused to kill all these people. He has got special affection for me. He would never kill me. If I do not offer myself, I would be considered disloyal and ungrateful. He stepped forward and said, "My protector, as all these people are meat eaters, they are not proper food for you. As it is, I am your natural food. I offer my body. Please kill me and satisfy your hunger. I shall consider myself fortunate for having sacrificed my life for my master."

As soon as the lion heard these words, he gestured to the others. The tiger, jackal and the wolf pounced on him and tore him to pieces. The foolish camel paid with his life for associating with and trusting the wicked and the cunning. Above all he emulated their example, failed to see through their treachery and so came to grief.

4. Never Fiddle with the Unknown

A businessman was having a temple constructed near his city. Lots of workers were engaged in the task doing different works. This story relates to the period when carpenters were engaged for woodwork. A big *Arjuna* tree was being sawn into planks. The workers used to go to the nearby city for lunch. That day, they all left to have their lunch. The carpenter had left a half sawn plank and had inserted a big wooden nail so that the two parts remained apart and the remaining part of the plank could be sawn easily when he resumed work.

A group of monkeys came there and started swinging on the trees. One of them sat on the plank. Monkeys by nature are playful. A monkey saw the wooden nail in the plank. For sometime, he looked curiously at it. Then he playfully tried to pull it out. He did not succeed at first and started pulling at it vigorously. The foolish monkey had no idea that his testicles were between the two sawn parts. As he pulled out the nail the two parts of the plank came together and his testicles were crushed between them. He screamed loudly and died instantaneously. The foolish monkey tried to fiddle with things that were beyond his comprehension and without thinking of the consequences. Anyone who does things like that is bound to meet with the same fate as that monkey.

❏ ❏ ❏

5. The Cunning Stork

There was a very large lake in the forest. It was full of fish of all varieties as also other marine lives. An old stork lived under a tree on the bank of the lake. He could not catch fish due to old age and was becoming weaker due to lack of food. He was pondering over his situation all the time. Then one day he hit upon a plan that would secure him food without much effort. He sat on the bank of the lake shedding copious tears. Seeing this a crab approached him and asked the reason. The crab inquired. "What is the matter with you? You are not even trying to catch fish and are weeping like this."

The stork replied, "Friend, I have sinned a lot in my life. I am fasting to atone for my sins. I was born in this lake, and have spent my whole life near it. I have heard a very disturbing news. Some astrologers have opined that there would be no rains for the next twelve years. This lake would soon dry up and all of you living in it will die. I love all of you who live here and cannot see you all die like this. Most of the creatures living in small ponds are shifting to bigger lakes with the help of their friends. The creatures living in this lake seem to be indifferent about the oncoming calamity. I am weeping for them. Everything will be over."

The crab told everyone about it. Everybody was scared but did not know how to cope with the problem. Eventually they all approached the stork to find a solution. The stork replied, "There is a huge lake at some distance from here. It is full of water and even if it does not rain for twenty years it will not dry up. If you desire, I can reach you to that lake one by one. I can take you riding on my back."

There was a regular brawl. Each creature wanted to go first. The crab was wise. He cautioned them, "The stork is a wily person. You should not trust him implicitly. He may have a trick under his sleeve. Nobody paid any attention to him. The stork started taking one fish at a time. He would take the fish to a rocky place and then throw it on the rocks and eat it up. In this way he ate up a number of fish. He would then return to take more, telling them stories about the abundance of water and food at the new place.

The crab still had his doubts. One day he came forward and said, "Uncle, you talked to me first about that lake. Why not take me there today?" The stork welcomed the suggestion. He had got fed up with eating fish everyday. He thought why not have change of diet. The crab jumped on the back of the stork and the stork flew off with the crab on its back. As the promised lake was not sighted for some time the crab grew suspicious. He also saw a lot of fish bones scattered all over the rocky terrain. He felt convinced that they had been duped.

The crab asked, "Uncle, when will we reach the lake?" The stork thought that the crab could not cause any harm and hence decided to tell him the truth. "Which lake are you talking about? I invented this story so that I could arrange my daily food without any trouble. I have killed all the fish that I brought. Your end is also near."

The crab retained his composure. As soon as he came to know the real intentions of the stork, he caught hold of the neck of the stork in his pincer-like legs. He started biting the neck with his sharp teeth till it was severed from the body. The crab reached the ground sticking to the stork's dead body. Then he slowly inched his way to the lake. He then narrated the story of the treachery of the stork to all the creatures of the lake. He told them how he was able to kill the stork and thanked God that he was alive to tell the tale. "There is not going to be any drought and you can live in the lake as before," he told them, "I was suspicious of his intentions from the very beginning but had to follow the opinion of the majority. It is truly said that truth can never be sifted in a crowd. You have seen that those who try to harm others by fraud meet a tragic end themselves."

❑ ❑ ❑

6. Fight between a Bird and an Elephant

A sparrow couple had a nest on a *tamal* tree. The female sparrow was sitting on her eggs while her male sat on a nearby branch keeping an eye over them. An elephant passed that way. As it was very hot the elephant came to rest under the same tree. After a while, he started eating the leaves of the overhanging branches. In the process he tore up many branches including the one on which the sparrow couple had made their nest. The nest fell to the ground and the eggs were smashed to pieces. The birds flew off to save their lives.

The female sparrow was in tears to see her eggs destroyed by the elephant. Hearing her wail, their woodpecker friend came to enquire about the commotion. The sparrow related the story of the destruction of their nest and eggs by the wild elephant. The woodpecker comforted them saying, "Whatever had to happen has come about. Weeping cannot mend matters. Try to bear your loss with fortitude." The male sparrow replied, "We understand that. The elephant has destroyed our eggs without rhyme or reason. You are our friend. We expect you to help us in punishing the elephant."

The woodpecker nodded in assent and said, "You are right. A friend in need is a friend indeed. If I do not come to your aid at the time of distress, I do not deserve to be called a friend. I shall call upon my friend Veenarav, the fly. Then we shall get together and find ways to punish the elephant."

The fly arrived and heard the story. She said, "We must do something. I shall call my friend Meghnad, a frog. Then we will plan our revenge." Meghnad arrived and assured them of his help. He opined that if they acted in unison, the elephant can be brought to his knees. He said, "Do as I tell you. The fly should get into the ear of the elephant and hum sweetly. The elephant would close his eyes to enjoy the music. The woodpecker should blind him with his sharp and long beak. The blind elephant would then start searching for water to quench his thirst. Now comes my part. I would sit near a deep pit with my friends croaking merrily. The elephant would think that he has reached a pond and will fall into the pit and die." Everyone played his part deftly and the elephant met his end.

❑ ❑ ❑

7. Dantil and Gorambh

I n the city of Vardhman in the eastern region, lived a
trader in ornaments and gems. His name was Dantil.
He was not only the favourite of the ruler, but the
ordinary people also looked upon him with respect
because of his good behaviour. The reason for the regard
was that he was an honest, pious and large-hearted
person. It is a common perception that you can be a
favourite only of the ruler or the common people. Dantil
was an exception as he enjoyed the confidence of both.

Dantil's daughter was getting married. Dantil invited
the ruler, his consort as well as the courtiers. The common
people were not forgotten either. Dantil received all with
warmth and hospitality. With the king and his queen
many attendants from the palace had also come. Amongst
them was a man named Gorambh who used to sweep
and clean the bedroom of the king. Because of his
proximity to the ruler, he thought himself to be an
important personage. Gorambh went and sat at a place
meant for the elite. Dantil saw him sitting there. He got
worried as he apprehended that the elite invitees might
not like his presence amongst them and get annoyed. At
first, he tried to persuade Gorambh to sit at the place
meant for people of his status. As Gorambh got adamant,
Dantil had him forcibly removed to where he thought he
belonged.

Gorambh was furious at being humiliated like this
and decided to take revenge. He would see to it that
Dantil fell from the King's favour. That would set him
right. He decided to wait for an opportune moment to
strike. Even an ant sometimes subdues an elephant.

Dantil could be brought to his knees if he made the right moves.

One day he was sweeping the room as the ruler lay on the bed. He started mumbling in a low voice as if he was talking to himself. "What an ungrateful person this fellow Dantil is. The ruler is so kind to him that he has allowed him unrestricted access to the palace and he is taking advantage of it. The wretched man is having an affair with the queen," he muttered under his breath. The ruler sat in the bed and asked, "Gorambh, is what you said just now true? Did you see it with your own eyes?"

Gorambh feigned drowsiness and said, "Did I say something? Please forgive me. I have been gambling whole night and did not get any sleep. I am so drowsy and hardly remember what I might have been talking."

Gorambh left the place soon after. The king was in great distress. He sat thinking that usually a man's innermost thoughts come out in a sleepy state. Gorambh might have seen something that was why he was talking like that. Women by nature were unstable. It is well known that even gods cannot know a man's destiny and a woman's nature. Only a fool can place implicit trust in them.

From that day entry of Dantil into the palace was prohibited. Dantil could not understand the reason for this unexpected turn of events. He had never hurt the king's or anyone else's interests. He thought that it was stupid to expect cleanliness in a crow or forgiveness in a snake. He felt a gambler would never be truthful. Who could expect patience in an impatient man or discretion in a drunkard. In the same way steadfast friendship, he thought, was alien to the nature of rulers. He decided to find out the reason for the king's displeasure.

He decided to see the king and sort out things. He reached the gates of the palace but the guards barred his entry. Gorambh was standing nearby. In a sarcastic tone he told the guards, "Do you realise whom you are stopping? Don't you know he is a favourite of the king. He would have you thrown out like me." Dantil immediately guessed that Gorambh was behind his discomfiture. He had treated him as an unimportant person but wise men have opined that even the servants of rulers, wealthy and influential people have some importance. They usually have the ears of their masters and turn them against you. He called Gorambh to his house in the evening and piled him with valuable gifts and feasted him. He told him, "I had no intention of humiliating you that day. There were certain social limitations and rules that were binding on all." Gorambh

31

was happy and assured him that he would undo what he had done out of pique. As it is you can always win over such persons by extending them some respect.

Next day, Gorambh went to the king's bedroom to clean it. He again started to talk to himself in a low voice. "Our king is a strange person. Imagine, he eats cucumber while easing himself in the morning." When the king heard this, he shouted at him, "What are you talking. When did you see me eating cucumber?" At this Gorambh rubbed his eyes and fell to the floor, "Forgive me my lord. I have again been gambling whole night. I might have been talking in a drowsy state."

Gorambh left the place profusely apologising for his conduct. The king sat thinking. Gorambh was accusing me of doing something that I have never done in my life. One should never believe a person of low status. Only fools like me do that. I doubted my loyal friend and my faithful wife by believing in this lowly person. Such people can never be trusted. He felt remorse at having wronged his friend Dantil and his own wife. He immediately called Dantil and apologised for his conduct saying that the misunderstanding had been removed. Dantil got back his previous position but could never know what Gorambh had done to denigrate him and how he made the king reverse his decision.

❏ ❏ ❏

8. Empty Vessels Make Much Noise

A jackal named Gomayu lived in some forest region. He could not find any food for many days and was extremely hungry. As he was wandering in the forest in search of food, he heard a strange noise. He had never heard such a sound in his life and wondered what it could be. At first, he hid himself behind a bush. Gathering courage, he approached the place from where the sound emanated.

He found a huge drum lying under a tree. It had been abandoned by an army that had fought a battle at that place. When a branch of the tree struck the side of the drum, it created a loud sound. His fear vanished as he saw no movement in the drum. It could be something full of food. Then he thought to himself, "It is better to make efforts than die of hunger like a coward." With pounding heart he struck at the drum with his hand. Nothing happened. He became certain that it contained food for many days. It could be some dead animal.

He started tearing at the cover of the drum. In the process he lost a few teeth. He eagerly jumped into the drum but found it empty. He was thoroughly disappointed and thought that those who act hastily without thinking of the consequences repent at leisure. The efforts that one puts in such action also get wasted.

❑ ❑ ❑

9. The Fake Vishnu

In ancient times, a youth named Kaulik lived in the province of Sindh. He was a weaver by profession. He had a childhood friend who was a carpenter. The carpenter was very proficient in his work and had deep knowledge about making mechanical things. Once, the two friends were wandering about in a fair near a temple. A lot of people had come to attend that fair. The princess of the realm also came astride an elephant. She was exceptionally beautiful with radiant complexion and large doe like eyes. As soon as Kaulik saw her he became completely besotted with her. He became unconscious and fell to the ground. His friend brought him back to his house. As he gained consciousness, he started wailing that he would die as he had fallen in love with the princess. He knew that she was beyond his reach and he could only pine away in her love. Powerful rulers would be her suitors.

The carpenter scolded him for his lack of manliness. He told him that one has to make efforts to gain one's objective. Men have conquered high seas and mountains by their efforts. If he desired the hand of the princess, he ought to try for it. Kaulik thought that his friend was making fun of him. He was aware of the disparity between his status and that of the princess. The carpenter asked him to be patient, and laid down a plan. He said he would give him a flying Garuda and make him up as God Vishnu. He would put two artificial arms on him. Made up as Vishnu, he could fly to the roof of the palace, meet her and seek her hand.

Kaulik protested that he would not deceive the princess like this. The carpenter countered that everything is fair in love and war. Made up as Vishnu, Kaulik flew on his wooden Garuda to the roof of the palace. He entered the bedroom of the princess and started stroking her silken hair. The princess woke up and found a stranger on her bed. In halting tones she asked as to who he was and how he got into her room. Kaulik feigned surprise at the question and said, "Don't you recognise me? I am Lord Vishnu. I have come to seek your hand in marriage. You do not remember that you were Radha in a previous birth when I came to earth as Krishna." The princess felt elated but asked him to see her father who would be delighted to meet him.

Kaulik felt that his well laid plan was going astray. He thought for a moment and said, "How can I appear before a mere mortal. I suggest that we undergo *Gandharva* marriage right now. If you hesitate, I shall destroy your entire family and kingdom." The princess trembled with fear and had no other option but to agree to the suggestion of the fake Vishnu. Kaulik continued his night visits to the bedroom of the princess unhindered. The attendants and maids of the palace got suspicious that some man came to the bedroom of the princess. They informed the ruler.

The ruler got worried, as is natural for any father, who had a beautiful daughter of marriageable age. He thought if the information was correct, it was a matter of grave concern. He knew that river and women have common nature. The river erodes both her banks. In the same way, a wayward daughter can damage her father's as well as her matrimonial family. The ruler talked to the queen, who straightaway went to the princess and asked, "There are rumours that a man comes to meet you every night."

The princess readily revealed the identity of the visitor. She told her that if they doubted her words they could see him from behind a screen. The Lord cannot appear before human beings. The king and the queen considered themselves as extremely lucky to have Lord Vishnu as their son-in-law. In the night, they saw Kaulik descending from his *Garuda* on the palace roof.

The king underwent a great change in his behaviour from that day. He became proud and arrogant. After all, he presumed, Lord Vishnu was his son-in-law. Who would dare to violate his boundaries or cast covetous eyes on his kingdom. He neglected his duties and started picking quarrels with his neighbouring states. He would attack them at will and occupy their lands. The rulers got together and decided to teach him a lesson. They gathered their armies and attacked his kingdom. The ruler found it difficult to face the combined armies of his neighbours and faced defeat.

He went to his daughter and said, "My daughter, you have to ask your husband Lord Vishnu to come to my aid or I shall lose my kingdom." When Kaulik came to see the princess in the night, she told him of his father's plight and requested him to destroy the armies of the attackers. Kaulik was scared. He might have assumed the appearance of Vishnu but could not get his qualities. If you cover yourself with a lion's skin you do not become a lion. He was a weaver. What did he know about conduct of war? But he had to do something for his beloved. Even if he was killed it did not matter. He told the princess that he would assist her father from the sky. Hearing this the king was assured of victory; who could defeat him when Vishnu would be there with his *sudarshan chakra*, he thought.

Next day, Kaulik prepared to take part in the battle astride his wooden *Garuda*. The real God Vishnu got worried in the heaven. He asked *Garuda* if he was aware of Kaulik's actions. *Garuda* said that he had been watching everything from the very beginning. What could be done if that foolish fellow was willingly courting death.

Lord Vishnu said, "You do not see the point *Garuda*. He is sure to be killed in the battle. The whole world will come to believe that Lord Vishnu died at the hands of mere mortals. Who would worship me after that? We have to save our reputation. I suggest that both of us enter the bodies of this fake Vishnu and *Garuda* and destroy the armies of the invading rulers." It did not take much time to vanquish the enemy forces and they took to their heels. The common people believed that the victory was due to the valour of the king's son-in-law.

As the invading armies retreated and fled, Kaulik descended from his wooden perch and stood before the king. He narrated the story of his deceit to the king and asked for his pardon. He also disclosed his real identity. The king was impressed by his honesty and courage and said, "You may be anyone but now you are my son-in-law and fully deserve to be one." He embraced Kaulik and married his daughter to him with due ceremonies and declared him to be his successor. The carpenter, Kaulik's friend, came to congratulate him and said, "Do you now believe that it is by efforts that one can gain his objective. Only the valiant get what they covet and even gods are forced to come to their aid."

10. The Story of a Crow and a Snake

A crow couple had a nest on a huge tree in the jungle. They were living a contented life. One day, a black snake came to live in the hollow of the tree. Now their troubles began. The snake would sneak into their nest and eat up their little ones and eggs when they went out in search of food. They were miserable but could not fight the snake. They approached the jackal living under the tree to advise them as to how they could get rid of the snake.

The wise jackal said, "You cannot get rid of your problems by worrying. Use your commonsense to kill the enemy." Then he told them a plan to finish off their enemy.

Next day, the crow flew to the palace. He found ladies of the palace bathing in a pool. Their jewellery was lying on the bank of the pool. The crow picked up a diamond necklace of the queen and flew away. The attendants of the palace chased him to retrieve the costly necklace. The crow threw the necklace into the hollow of the tree where the snake lived. The servants saw him dropping it there. As they peeped into the hollow they found the snake coiled inside. They killed the snake and picked up the necklace. Thus the crow was able to liquidate his enemy.

11. Tit for Tat

A trader named Jeerndhan lived in some city. Once he was a very affluent person leading a comfortable life. His luck changed and he lost all his money and wealth. It was distressing for him as with loss of wealth people did not respect him as before. Hence, he decided to go to some other place to try his luck. He had a weighing scale of antique value. It was a sort of family heirloom. There was none like it in the entire region.

He went to a moneylender and pawned the weighing scale with him. With that money he moved to another city to earn money. It so happened that he did better in the new place and earned a lot of money. He returned to his native place and approached the moneylender, "Sethji, I have come to repay the loan. Please give me back my weighing scale."

The moneylender did not want to part with the valuable scale. He pulled a long face and in a sad voice told the trader, "I am really very sorry. I am afraid I cannot give back your weighing scale. In your absence, it was eaten up by rats." Jeerndhan could see through the falsehood but he controlled himself and decided to teach the moneylender a lesson. He replied, "Lalaji, forget about it. It is not your fault if the rats made a meal of it. As it is, nothing in this world can last for ever. Anyway, I wish to have my bath in the river. Please ask your son to accompany me so that he can look after my belongings while I bathe in the river."

The moneylender was happy to be let off so easily. The precious weighing scale would now be his for ever. He called his son Dhandev and asked him to accompany

41

Jeerndhan to the river. Jeerndhan had his bath. He then took the son of the moneylender to a cave under some false pretext. He left the boy in the cave and then blocked the entrance with a huge rock.

Then he hurried to the house of the moneylender. He posed to be greatly agitated. Seeing him alone, the moneylender enquired about his son. In a very sad voice, Jeerndhan said, "Sethji, I do not know how to break the sad news. A hawk pounced on your son and flew away with him as he sat on the river bank."

The moneylender was beside with rage. "Do you take me to be an utter fool. Are you in your senses. How can a hawk fly away with a child? Bring him to me forthwith or I shall take you to the court," he shouted in a loud voice. Jeerndhan calmly replied, "Lala, nothing is impossible in this world. If rats can eat a steel weighing scale, then what is surprising if a hawk lifted a child and flew away. If you want your son to return, give me my weighing scale."

The moneylender rushed to the court and lodged a complaint against the trader. He alleged that his son had been abducted by him. The judge looked at the trader and sought his explanation. The trader said, "My lord, what could I do? The hawk picked up the child and flew away. I chased it for some distance but then lost sight of it. Now, how can I restore his son?"

The judge admonished the trader, "Who can believe your cock and bull story? It is unbelievable. Whoever heard of a hawk lift a healthy boy and fly away with him." The trader humbly submitted, "Your Honour, if rats can eat a steel weighing scale, then what is so strange in a hawk flying away with a child." The judge looked perplexed and asked him to tell the entire story. He smiled as the trader narrated the entire story. He took little time to order that the moneylender should return the weighing scale while the trader would restore the son.

❑ ❑ ❑

12. The Golden-hearted Thief

A very learned brahmin lived in some city. Though he was a very learned person, he could not resist stealing things. Maybe, this was due to after-effects of misdeeds committed in his previous birth. One day, he saw four wealthy brahmins arrive in his city. They were traders who had a lot of money on them. They had come to that city to sell their goods. The thief brahmin started making plans to deprive them of their possessions.

Eventually, he hit upon a plan. He met them and impressed them with his vast learning and gentle behaviour. They allowed him to stay with them. The thief brahmin served the four businessmen with sincerity and devotion. As they say, a woman of loose morals poses to be very coy. Salty water is always cooler and a crook is generally sweet-tongued.

The four brahmin businessmen were able to sell all their goods at good profit. They purchased precious stones and gems with that money. They also decided to return to their native place. As dacoits were common on highways and forest areas, they hid their precious stones and gems inside their thighs. The thief brahmin saw all this. He had been unable to steal anything of value. He thought all his labour in serving the businessmen had gone to waste. Hence, he implored them to take him with them. He planned that at an opportune moment he would poison them and take away the jewels.

As they proceeded on their journey, they went to a village inhabited by *bhils* who looted wayfarers. These *bhils* had trained the crows of their village to signal them if the travellers had money with them. The crows signalled to the *bhils* that these brahmins had a lot of wealth with them.

On getting clear signals from the crows the *bhils* surrounded the five brahmins and asked them to give up all they had. The brahmins denied that they had any money. They told the *bhils* that they were poor brahmins who lived on the generosity of their clients. The *bhils* beat them up and searched for the money. They did not find anything on them. They were surprised as their crows had never failed them. They told the brahmins to hand over their money otherwise they would be forced to be harsh with them. They said, "If you have hidden your wealth inside your bodies, we shall cut you up limb by limb. We shall find it and hence it is better for you to hand it over willingly and avoid death."

As the thief brahmin heard this he thought that the *bhils* would not let them go alive. After the four his turn would also come and he would be killed. So why not save the lives of these four by giving up my own life. He approached the *bhils* and said, "You seem to have so much faith in your crows. You can cut me up and see that we have not hidden anything inside our bodies." The *bhils* cut up the brahmin but did not find a single penny on him. They were convinced that their crows had made a mistake this time. They freed the four brahmins. The brahmins thanked their stars and hurriedly left the place. They felt a sense of deep gratitude for the thief brahmin who had laid down his life to save them. They felt that it is rightly said that it is better to have a learned enemy than a foolish friend. A wise enemy is less dangerous than a foolish friend who may cause harm with his thoughtless actions.

13. A Stitch in Time Saves Nine

Three fish named Anagat Vidhata, Pratyunmati and Yadbhavishya lived in a lake with their families and relations. One day, some fishermen passed by seeing a lot of fish in that lake. They decided to cast their nets in that lake the following day. When Anagat Vidhata heard them, he called all the fish and said, "You have heard the fishermen. I advise that we move to some other lake before they arrive in the morning. It is said that the weak should save their lives by running away rather than face a strong adversary." Pratyunmati agreed and asked his family and relations to abandon the lake.

Yadbhavishya made fun of them and said, "Why should we leave this place. We have lived here for generations. If death is ordained, it will catch us wherever we go. I shall not leave." Seeing him adamant, others left. The next day the fishermen cast their nets in that lake. Yadbhavishya and his entire clan perished because of his foolhardiness.

14. The Pewit Couple and Sea

A pewit couple lived near the sea. The female pewit became pregnant and asked her male to look for a safe place for her delivery. The male replied, "This place near the sea is clean and beautiful. Why should we go elsewhere?" The female pewit countered, "How can my eggs be safe here? Even elephants are washed away when the sea is in high tide." The male pewit had an exaggerated notion about his prowess. He thought it would be cowardice to abandon the place. Then he felt he was strong enough to teach the sea a lesson if he dared to harm the eggs.

The sea smiled at this bragging of the tiny pewit. He decided to teach a lesson to the pewit. The female pewit lay her eggs near the sea. One day, when the pewit couple went out in search of food, the sea waves rose and took away their eggs. The female pewit burst into tears as she found her eggs missing. She blamed her husband for the tragedy for she had forewarned him but he did not pay any heed to her advice. But the male pewit, who had an inflated ego, said, "The sea will have to suffer for his misdeed. I shall dry up the sea with my beak. The sea does not know my strength." The female pewit remained unconvinced. She opined that the sea was so vast that his small beak could never accomplish the task.

The male pewit assured her, "I know the sea is vast and powerful. My cause is just. Have you not seen the powerful elephant being controlled by a small iron hook. Men are known to have subdued its waves and travelled all over on the seas. Size does not make you invincible. It would be extreme cowardice not to punish the sea for its mean act." The female pewit advised that it would be better to fight the sea with the help of friends. It is said that if the weak get united, they become invincible.

The pewit called all the birds for a conference and related the story of the sea's vile act. In no time, crores of birds assembled at the sea shore to dry up the sea. Soon they realised that the task was uphill. After all, hundreds of mighty rivers empty themselves into the sea. Eventually, the pewit approached *Garuda,* the king of the bird kingdom and asked him to punish the sea. Garuda was quite capable of doing it. But he could not take any action as sea was under the protection of his master Lord Vishnu.

By coincidence, a messenger arrived asking Garuda to immediately report to Lord Vishnu as He needed his services for going somewhere. Garuda saw his opportunity to help the pewit. He sent back the messenger with the message that he had no desire to serve Lord Vishnu any more. He added that a master who did not care to look into the problems of his attendants did not deserve to be served.

When the messenger conveyed all this to Lord Vishnu, He decided to see Garuda personally to find out the reason for his displeasure. Garuda related the tale of sea's misdemeanour. The Lord immediately hastened to the sea shore and admonished the sea. He said, "One who terrorises the weak because of his strength and power is called a tyrant. If such a tyrant is not punished, it leads to anarchy and disintegration of established order. It did not behove you to take away the eggs of the pewit couple. I ask you to return the eggs and apologise to them for your arrogance. If you do not do that, prepare yourself for punishment at my hands."

As he heard the Lord's threat, the sea fell at his feet. He returned the eggs and apologised to the pewit couple. The pewit couple forgave him. The sea had to suffer this humiliation as he thought that the pewit couple were too insignificant forgetting that many times the weak triumph over the strong and powerful.

❑ ❑ ❑

15. Suchimukh and a Group of Monkeys

Wise men have opined that one should not give advice to fools, vicious and short-tempered people as the advisor runs the risk of coming to grief. This story

amply proves the futility of rendering advice to such people.

A group of monkeys lived in a hilly region. During the cold winter season, rains made matters worse. The monkeys were shivering with cold and did not know how to warm themselves. Suddenly they saw a heap of red flowers under a tree. They gathered round it to warm themselves. They had seen human beings sitting round red objects and warming themselves. They foolishly believed that the red flowers would provide warmth.

A bird named Suchimukh saw it from the tree. "Friends," he said, "This is not fire but wild red flowers. You cannot get any warmth from them. The clouds are getting denser and it may rain heavily. I advise you to find some cave to protect yourself from the biting cold and rain."

The leader of the monkeys replied, "You foolish bird. You think you are very wise. Go away or keep your mouth shut." Suchimukh again said, "I do not claim to know much but I can tell you these flowers will not ward off your cold." The monkeys got irritated with the bird's chatter. They asked her to keep quiet, as she was adding to their troubles with constant nagging.

Suchimukh once again made an effort to make them see reason. But monkeys are monkeys. "It seems you will not stop bothering us," so saying a young monkey climbed the tree and caught hold of Suchimukh. He plucked her feathers and threw her down on the rocks. They kept sitting round the flowers. Many died in the hailstorm, others were injured before some could find shelter amongst the rocks.

❑ ❑ ❑

16. Dharmbuddhi and Papbuddhi

Dharmbuddhi and Papbuddhi were close friends living in some city. Both of them were very poor. One day, they both decided to try their luck in some foreign land. Maybe, they would be able to earn enough money elsewhere which would be handy for a comfortable life in old age. As luck would have it, they

were successful in earning a lot of money and decided to return to their native place. Papbuddhi was a man of evil nature. He planned to dupe his friend of his share of the money. As they neared their native place, he counselled, "Friend, we should not take the entire money to our place. It is better to hide it in this forest. We have got a lot of relations who would expect us to help them. We can come and dig it up as and when we need it."

Dharmbuddhi was a man of simple nature. He fell for the trap. He readily agreed as he thought that it was their hard earned money and they alone were entitled to enjoy it. They dug a pit under a tree and hid the money. Then they proceeded to their respective places. After a few days, Papbuddhi went to the forest and dug out all the money. He then covered the pit and returned to his house. One day, he went to Dharmbuddhi and said, "Friend, I have used up all the money I had. Let us go to the forest and bring some more." Dharmbuddhi readily accompanied him. When they dug up the place they found the vessel in which they had kept the money totally empty. Papbuddhi started beating his head at the loss. Then he turned round and accused Dharmbuddhi of stealing the money as he was the only person who knew the exact spot where the money had been hidden. Dharmbuddhi protested that he could not even dream of committing such an unpardonable sin. They started quarrelling and the matter went to the court, where both accused each other of stealing it.

The judge listened to their stories and opined that since there were no witnesses or documents in the case, it will have to be decided by divine test. Papbuddhi protested, "This is not the correct procedure. In the absence of documents you should examine witnesses. In my case, the tree under which the money was hidden is a witness. Let us examine it." The judge decided to go to the site to take the evidence of the tree on the following day.

Papbuddhi returned to his house and told his father, "I have stolen Dharmbuddhi's share of money. The matter is before the court. I can be saved if you help me or I may face death sentence." The father was no better than the son. Papbuddhi unfolded his plan to him. The father had to hide in the hollow of the tree and speak as directed.

Next day, Dharmbuddhi and Papbuddhi went to the site with the judge. There Papbuddhi declared, "The gods are witness to all that we men do. Tree god, name the thief who has stolen the money." Papbuddhi's father, who was sitting in the hollow of the tree, immediately spoke up, "It is Dharmbuddhi who took out the money." Everyone was surprised but Dharmbuddhi suspected that some trick had been played. As the judge got busy in pronouncing the judgement, he collected dry grass and firewood and put them in the hollow of the tree. Then he set fire to them.

Sitting there, Papbuddhi's father became nervous. When it became too hot, he tumbled out of the tree. He was badly scolded. He then related the entire story to the judge who ordered Papbuddhi to be hanged from the same tree. His share of money was also given to Dharmbuddhi. However cleaver a dishonest man and a sinner may think of himself, his sin catches up with him in the end. Crime never pays and truth always triumphs.

17. The Wise Rabbit

A very powerful lion named Bhasurak lived in a forest. Being very proud of his strength, he recklessly killed a lot of animals. The animals living in that forest were sick of his cruel ways. They got together to find a solution to this reign of terror. Ultimately, they met Bhasurak and told him, "O' Mighty King, you need not kill so many animals everyday. We have decided that one amongst us will present himself daily whom you can kill to satisfy your hunger. It will stop unnecessary killings and save you the botheration of hunting." Bhasurak accepted the proposal.

From that day the animals of the forest moved about fearlessly. Each day they selected one of them to be sent to the lion. One day it was the turn of a rabbit. He was naturally terrified at the thought of his imminent death. He proceeded to the lion's den thinking about how to get rid of this cruel lion and save his fellow animals. In a playful mood, he peeped into a well which came his way. He saw his own reflection in the water. Immediately a scheme to do away with the lion flashed past his mind.

He slowed his pace and reached the lion's den by the evening. Bhasurak was pacing in front of his den. He was very hungry. He roared as the rabbit approached him. He said, "So today they have sent you. How can a tiny animal like you satisfy my hunger? Then you have come so late. It seems I will have to kill all the animals of the forest as punishment." The rabbit bowed respectfully and requested him to listen to the reason for his being late. He then haltingly said, "The animals are not at fault. Five of us were sent for you today. On the way, another lion barred our way and enquired where we were headed to. We told him that we were on our way to the lion king Bhasurak as his food.

"At this that lion became furious. He said, 'Who is this Bhasurak. I am the king of this forest. I shall tear him from limb to limb. Bring him here and I shall show him who is more powerful'." So saying he killed and ate my four companions. He then asked me to go to you and warn you to leave this forest forthwith or face his wrath.

Bhasurak was beside with anger. He commanded the rabbit to take him to that lion. He would not rest till he had killed that imposter who had dared to challenge his might. The rabbit meekly said, "My lord, it behoves the valiant to fight for their rights. That is the way of the brave. But, the other lion has a fortified den. It may be difficult for you to fight him in his den." Bhasurak laughed and said, "You need not worry. Simply take me to his place and I shall prove who is more powerful."

The rabbit was elated. He saw his plan succeeding. He took Bhasurak to the well where he had seen his own reflection in the water. He looked around and said,

"It seems that the coward has gone and hid himself in his den. Come with me. I shall show you where he lives." He peeped into the well and told the lion that his enemy was hiding there.

Bhasurak peeped into the well. He saw his reflection in it. He presumed it was the other lion who had challenged his authority. "Come out you coward," he roared. His own words came back as echo from the well. In a fit of anger, he jumped into the well and was drowned.

The rabbit was beside with joy and rushed to the forest to convey the glad tidings. The animals danced round the clever rabbit proclaiming that intellect was always superior to animal strength. The little fellow had amply proved it.

18. The Greedy Hermit

There was a monastery in an unpopulated area. Many monks lived there. Amongst them was a hermit named Dev Sharma. He had collected a lot of money from the offerings made at temple. Dev Sharma was a greedy person. He did not trust anybody and was always worried about the safety of his wealth which he kept in a bag. He never parted with that bag and always kept it on his person.

It is rightly said that money is a source of misery at every stage. First, you suffer a lot in earning and accumulating it. Then it is painful when you have to spend it. Above all is the problem of keeping it safe from thieves. In this case also, a thief named Ashadbhuti had his eyes on this money. He made many efforts to get at it but could not succeed. The walls of the monastery were very strong and entrance into it was well nigh impossible. He decided that he could steal this money by tricking the hermit. Eventually, he decided to follow the path of deception that all crooked men adopt to cheat others.

He went to see Dev Sharma disguised as a *sadhu*. He expressed his desire to be his disciple and gain knowledge at his feet. He told Dev Sharma that he felt that everything in this world was illusory and bound to perish. He wanted to be free from the cycle of rebirths. Taking him to be an earnest seeker, Dev Sharma accepted him as his disciple. He told him that he can gain his objective by repeating Shiva-mantra. He also allowed him to build a hut for himself at the entrance of the monastery.

Ashadbhuti left no stone unturned in serving Dev Sharma. He looked after all his needs and listened to his teachings with rapt attention. In no time, he gained the full confidence of his teacher. At the same time, he was looking for an opportunity to grab the bag. It so happened that Dev Sharma got an invitation from a disciple to visit his house and also feast at his place.

Dev Sharma left the monastery with Ashadbhuti to go to his disciple's place. As usual, the bag containing his wealth was with him. As they reached a river, Dev Sharma told Ashadbhuti, "Son, you wait here and look after my clothes. I will take my bath and then we will proceed further." Ashadbhuti's joy had no limits. He thought now is the time to steal the bag. He told the hermit to take his time as he would be there to guard his possessions. As soon as Dev Sharma was out of sight, he picked the bag and hastily left the place.

Dev Sharma sat behind a bush to ease himself at a little distance. There he saw a strange sight. Two rams were fighting each other. As they rammed each other with their heads, blood oozed out of their foreheads. As soon as they retraced their steps to clash again with force, a jackal rushed forward to lick the blood off their foreheads. Dev Sharma thought that the jackal was such a fool. He did not realise the risk he was taking. If he got caught between the warring rams, he was sure to be crushed to death. Then it happened. The jackal was caught between the fighting rams and lost his life.

Thinking about the foolish jackal, Dev Sharma came to the river bank. He found Ashadbhuti missing along with his clothes and the bag of money. He started wailing loudly and became unconscious unable to bear the loss of his entire possession. When he regained consciousness, he realised that he was more foolish than the jackal whom he had seen losing his life a short while ago. He had lost the earnings of a lifetime as he foolishly placed his trust in a stranger. He realised that one should be guided by his mind in distinguishing between good and bad, proper and improper and not be led away by the dictates of heart. He started in search of Ashadbhuti as he regained his composure. He followed the footprints of that cheat so that he could get at him and regain his money.

19. The Blue Jackal

A jackal named Chandarav lived in a forest. Wandering about for finding some food, he strayed into a nearby village. As soon as the dogs of the village espied him, they chased him. The jackal ran for his life and entered the house of a washerman to protect himself from the dogs. In his state of fright, he fell into a huge tub full of blue colour that the washerman had kept to dye clothes. The dogs left as they saw him falling into the tub. When he felt secure that there were no dogs around, he came out. But, now the jackal was completely dyed in blue colour. He was surprised that the dogs did not pay any attention to him. Rather they started fleeing as they saw the blue complexioned jackal.

The jackal made a quick exit and ran towards the forest. When he reached the forest, he found that most of the animals seemed to be afraid of him. That was natural as they had never seen any animal of that colour. They took him to be some strange animal. Even lions, tiger, wolves and other wild beasts avoided him not knowing the nature and strength of this strange animal. Chandarav guessed that he would take advantage of this coloured appearance and formulated a plan to make the best of the situation.

The animals of the forest called for a meeting to discuss the appearance of this strange animal. The lion addressed the gathered denizens of the forest, "Friends, a strange animal has entered our forest. We know nothing about its nature or strength. The wise have opined that one should keep a distance from anyone or thing about whose nature or strength you are ignorant. Friendship

or enmity with such a person is bound to invite disaster."
All the animals agreed with the lion's observations.

Chandarav was observing this from a distance. He stepped forward and addressed them, "Why are you all so afraid of me. There is nothing to be scared of. I am Kukudadrum. Lord Brahma has sent me here as your ruler. Hence, from now onwards accept me as your ruler and obey me." The animals consulted amongst themselves and decided to accept him as the new king. The crafty jackal appointed lion as his prime minister. The tiger became his bodyguard whereas wolf became his sentry. He took care not to have anything to do with his fellow jackals. Rather he banished them from his kingdom. The wolves chased them out. From that day, lions, the tiger and others brought the killed preys to him and he would distribute the meat amongst them keeping the best part for himself. Thus he led a life of ease and authority.

The humiliated jackals were miserable. They were condemned to a life of exile. They were anxious to find a way to end the rule of this fraud. An old jackal opined that Kukudadrum seemed to be a jackal. The others expressed surprise that being of the same species he had treated his own people so cruelly. The old jackal replied, "When a lowly person gets into some high position much above his capabilities, he would always try to keep away from his own people to prove his high pedigree. I suggest that you howl collectively. If he is a jackal, he will not be able to resist his innate nature and is sure to immediately respond by howling."

One day when Chandarav was sitting with his courtiers, the jackals started howling collectively. Chandarav forgot that he was sitting there as their king. He could not resist the urge to howl with the jackals. Hearing his voice, the animals realised that they had been duped by a mere jackal. The lion and the tiger pounced on him and tore him apart. The moral of the story is that one should not ignore or displease one's own people once he becomes powerful, for they are bound to feel aggrieved and would plot one's downfall as happened in the case of Chandarav.

Part-II

MITRASAMPRAPTI

As he finished the first part, Acharya Vishnu Sharma told the princes that he would now instruct them about the ways of the wise and the learned who achieve their objectives despite limitations and lack of resources. Sincere friends, though rare, are able to help one another get over their difficulties.

1. The Unlucky Weaver

A weaver named Saumalik lived in some city. He was an excellent craftsman and clothes woven by him were the best in the market. Still he never had any spare money. He eked out his living with difficulty. On the other hand, many weavers, whose work was of inferior quality, were very prosperous. One day, he told his wife that he wished to shift to some other place as his native place somehow did not suit him. His wife told him that one can never hope to get anything that is not ordained for him. She opined that age, wealth, learning and death are determined when you are in the womb and nothing can change them. Saumalik was adamant and decided to try his luck in the city of Vardhman. Being industrious, he worked hard for three years and was able to save a thousand gold coins.

He decided to return to his native place. It got dark in the way. He climbed to the branch of a big tree and lay down to sleep. He dreamt that two divine figures were talking to each other. One said, "You very well know that this man is fated to have money sufficient for his needs. Why have you given him so much wealth." The other replied, "I had to reward him for his industry. Whether he is able to use it is in your hands." Saumalik got up with a start and reached for his bag of gold. The gold coins were not there. He felt miserable. He did not have anything to show his wife as reward for his three years of hard work.

He decided to return to Vardhman city. This time he could save five hundred gold coins in a year. He set out for his native city. This time he did not stop on the way.

After some time, he found the same divine figures approaching him. One said, "You have again given this man five hundred gold coins which was not his destiny." The other replied, "I had to give him compensation for his hard work. You control fate. The final decision is in your hands." Getting anxious, Saumalik felt his bag and found it empty. He felt dejected and thought of ending his life. How could he face his wife? He made a rope and tying one end to the tree he put the loop round his neck to die.

One of the divine figures appeared and said, "Do not kill yourself. It was I who stole your money. It is not in your destiny to have extra money. You return to your home. I have decided to grant you a boon." Saumalik replied, "If you want to grant me a boon, then let me have more money." The divine figure said, "I can give you enormous wealth. That will not be of any use to you. It is ordained that you can neither use it nor enjoy it." Saumalik countered that it did not matter. Society respects the wealthy. The divine figure then suggested, "You return to Vardhman city. Two brothers named Guptadhan and Upbhuktadhan live there. You meet them and then tell me if you want to be rich like Guptadhan or Upbhuktadhan. I shall grant your wish according to your choice."

Saumalik returned to Vardhman. First he went to the place of Guptadhan. It was nearly dark as he reached his house. Guptadhan and his family asked him what he wanted. "I am a traveller and want shelter and food for the night," Saumalik told them. Guptadhan shouted at him, "My house is not an inn. I have no food for vagabonds like you. You go away from my house." Ignoring the insult, Saumalik lay down in a corner. He was given a little food.

In the night, Saumalik saw the same divine figures in his dream. One was saying, "Guptadhan was not supposed to spend any money on this man but he has done so." The other replied, "It was my duty to provide food and shelter to Saumalik who stayed back even after being humiliated. The fate of Guptadhan is in your hands. You do whatever you desire." Next day, when Saumalik rose to leave, he learnt that Guptadhan had fallen ill. Thus the little money that he spent on Saumalik was adjusted as he went without food due to illness.

Saumalik left for the house of Upbhuktadhan. He was received warmly and provided all comforts. Upbhuktadhan fed him lavishly though he had to buy things on credit. Saumalik went to sleep on a clean and comfortable bed. The two divine figures again appeared in his dream. One said, "You have made Upbhuktadhan spend so much money on Saumalik. He had to take a loan for it. How is he supposed to repay it." The other replied, "I rewarded Saumalik for his effort to pluck a mango and a jack fruit. One fruit hardly satisfies the hunger while the other can for many days. How Upbhuktadhan repays the loan is your problem."

In the morning, Saumalik got up to leave. He saw an officer of the king giving money to Upbhuktadhan saying that the ruler liked his artistic creations and has sent this money as reward. Both the divine figures appeared before Saumalik and asked, "Now tell us which type of wealth you require." Saumalik bowed to them and said, "The money that cannot feed a hungry person or give shelter to a traveller is useless. It makes a man behave like an animal. I do not need such wealth. I would like to have money like that of Upbhuktadhan."

The divine figure that controlled fate said, "You have asked for a boon in consonance with your destiny. I grant that you will never be short of money. From now on, your efforts will attract better returns."

Saumalik returned to his home. Immediately, he got an order to make dresses for the princess who was getting married. His dresses were liked and the king rewarded him generously for his exquisite work. Saumalik built a house for himself and sunk a well for people at large. A businessman happened to drink at his well and hearing of his good craftsmanship placed orders worth millions. Saumalik utilised the extra money in constructing roads, schools and in other social welfare activities. He distributed it amongst his needy relations and poor people. He knew that the money would not remain with him and hence it was best utilised for the well-being of the people.

❑ ❑ ❑

2. Greed Never Pays

A hunter roamed about in a forest for some prey. He espied a black wild boar and taking aim released the arrow. The arrow pierced the boar. He was enraged at this attack. Instead of running away he turned round and attacked the hunter. He tore open the stomach of the hunter. Eventually both died of their injuries.

After some time a jackal passed that way. As soon as he saw the dead hunter and the boar, he was beside himself with joy. He thanked Providence for providing him food for many days. It is rightly said that even if you do not make any efforts, the good and bad effects of your previous life's deeds devolve on you. He looked around and found the bow lying on the ground. The string of the bow was made of the intestines of some animal. The jackal decided to start eating with the bowstring. It snapped as the jackal gnawed at it with his sharp teeth. The other end of the bow hit the jackal with force of such intensity that it pierced the jackal's skull and knocked it out. Extra greed and excessive avarice cost the jackal his life.

❏ ❏ ❏

3. The Suspect Exchange

A brahmin couple lived in a village. They were extremely poor. It was with great difficulty that the brahmin was able to keep his body and soul together. His wife was always taunting him for his poverty. She grumbled that they never had two square meals a day. She said, "Since marriage, I have never known any comforts. I never had any jewellery or good clothes." The brahmin replied that it was enough that they could eat. He advised her to be content with her situation.

As they were arguing in this way, a sadhu arrived at their house and asked for some food. The brahmin told his wife, "I am going to another village for alms. It is *makar sankranti*. You feed this sadhu." The wife realised that there was no food in the house that she could offer to the guest. Then she remembered that there were some sesame seeds. She cleaned them and pounded them and spread them to dry. Misfortunes never come alone. As luck would have it, a dog came and pissed on the spread-out sesame seeds.

The woman felt miserable. She could not feed the guest with the soiled seeds. She hit upon a plan. She took the seeds in a basket and made rounds of the city calling, "Exchange cleaned and pounded sesame seeds with equal weight of uncleaned seeds." Hearing this, a housewife thought that it was a good bargain. She would be saved the trouble of cleaning and pounding. She came out and invited the brahmin woman inside the house. At that time her son came out and said, "Mother, do not do it. Only a mad person would exchange her cleaned sesame seeds with uncleaned ones. There must be some snag in it. Nobody gives good quality things for bad quality ones." The mother accepted the advice and went into the house.

❑ ❑ ❑

4. Searching for Friends

There was a city called Mahilaropya in some district of the southern peninsula. A little away from this city was a huge banyan tree which gave shelter to a lot of birds of all kinds. A crow, named Laghupatnak also lived on that tree. One day he set out in search of food. He saw a hunter coming towards the banyan tree with a strong net and a bag of rice. The crow became anxious about the safety of the innumerable residents of the tree and came back. He cautioned all the birds not to fall prey to greed and get down to eat the rice. As expected the hunter laid his net under the tree and sprinkled grains of rice all over it. He then hid himself behind a bush waiting for the birds to get down to eat the rice.

The feathered community of the tree did not get down as they had been warned about their entrapment. A group of pigeons led by their chief Chitragreev passed that way. Though Laghupatnak warned them about the hunter, being very hungry, they ignored his advice. More than fifty pigeons including their leader Chitragreev were entrapped in the net. The hunter was elated to find so many birds in his net. The pigeons were panicky and did not know what to do. Their chief Chitragreev addressed them, "Friends, it is of no use to rue now. Whatever had to happen has come about. Now we have to act unitedly to get over the problem. It is said that if a person does not lose his cool when beset with problems will eventually surmount them. Let us all fly away with the net and then we will think about how to get out of it."

As the hunter approached them, the pigeons flew away with the net with all their combined strength. The hunter was aghast and chased them for some time. He thought that as the pigeons would get tired they would come down. But soon he lost sight of them. Laghupatnak followed the pigeons as he was curious to find as to how they would free themselves from the net.

When Chitragreev saw that the hunter was nowhere in sight, he asked the pigeons to fly towards north-east of the city where his friend Hiranyak, the mouse, lived in his fortified burrows. They got down at the residence of Hiranyak. Chitragreev called out for his friend. Recognising the voice of his friend, Hiranyak came out and expressed surprise at the plight of his friend and his followers. Chitragreev narrated the entire story and said, "We are in trouble because of our greed. It is well known that greed diverts one of prudence. Now please cut this net and free us of this bondage." Hiranyak wanted to free his friend first. Chitragreev protested and requested him to free his followers first. He said, "They are my dependants. It is my duty to look after them. A leader should care for his loyal followers before he thinks of himself. A leader who cares more for his followers earns their eternal loyalty." Hiranyak took no time in cutting the net with his sharp teeth. Soon Chitragreev flew away with his horde.

Laghupatnak saw and heard all the talks between Chitragreev and Hiranyak. He was very impressed. He thought that it was difficult to come across such true friends. I would be lucky if I can find such friends. He went to the door of the burrow and called for Hiranyak. Hiranyak did not come out and asked from inside his fort what he wanted. The crow replied, "I am Laghupatnak. I want to be your friend." Hiranyak countered, "This is against the law of nature. I am your natural prey. How can we be friends? Please go away from here."

Laghupatnak made another effort. He said, "It is not necessary that every creature should act according to his natural inclination and instincts. There can be exceptions. I have been immensely impressed by what I saw and heard just now. Please honour me with your friendship." Hiranyak replied, "Inborn tendencies are hard to shed. Fire can never be cool. If one develops enmity due to some temporary cause, it can be ended. Ours is natural and inborn enmity that cannot be wished away. How can I trust you?" The crow suggested that he remained inside his burrow and even then they could be friends. The mouse thought for a while and said, "You will remain outside and I can talk to you from inside my hole." Laghupatnak agreed and they started exchanging their views from their respective positions. Laghupatnak also started bringing food for his friend.

Gradually they became fast friends. The mouse did not hesitate to come out and sit under the wings of the crow. One day Laghupatnak seemed to be in a sad mood as he came to see his friend. Hiranyak enquired about the cause of his feeling of misery. Laghupatnak told him that he was leaving the place. Hiranyak was dumbstruck. He had become so fond of the crow that he could not think of life without his living in that forest. He said, "The ruler of this place is lazy and a debauch. He is only interested in adding on to his harem. The learned and good people are leaving this kingdom. The ruler is surrounded by sycophants and the whole social system has collapsed. Even the nature is offended and the crops are failing. People are hungry and are killing birds for food. Life is so insecure. It is no use living in such a place."

"Where do you intend going?" Hiranyak enquired. Laghupatnak said, "There is a huge pond towards the south of this city. My friend, Mantharak lives there. He will help me in finding food." The mouse then expressed his desire to go with him. Hiranyak said that he was also disenchanted with that place. And that he would tell him the reasons later. Laghupatnak accepted this proposal. He asked the mouse to sit on his back and he flew in the direction of the pond, which they reached in a few days.

Mantharak, the tortoise, did not recognise his friend at first glance. He dived into the pond. Laghupatnak asked the mouse to alight and called out for his friend. Mantharak came out and greeted his friend warmly. Hiranyak came forward and was introduced to Mantharak. Laghupatnak praised Hiranyak and told Mantharak about his innumerable qualities of head and heart. He also disclosed that due to some reasons he got sick of his people and place and desired to live with them. Mantharak asked him the reason and Hiranyak related his tale of woes.

Mantharak sympathised with him and said, "Friend, this world is a cruel place. How can you expect sacrifice, affection and love in this selfish world? You cannot find anybody who has not been treated like you. Do not grieve over the past. You are welcome to live with us." The three friends started living together.

One day, as they sat talking, a deer arrived. He seemed to be scared of something and was looking back over his shoulders. Laghupatnak accosted him and asked the reason for his nervousness. The deer answered, "Is there any place where I can hide? A hunter is after me." Laghupatnak looked around and said, "You need not fear anymore. The hunter is nowhere in sight." The deer told them that he has got separated from his herd. Laghupatnak invited him to stay with them. Chitrang, the deer, gratefully accepted the invitation. The four became inseparable and their days passed in one another's company.

Sometime later, a jackal named Lubdhak also arrived there. As he saw Chitrang, he thought the meat of this well built deer would be so delicious. He realised that he could not kill him and would have to plot his liquidation. He started talking to Chitrang very sweetly and requested the foursome to include him in their circle. At this, Mantharak said, "You are a meat-eating animal. Then your wily nature and ways are well known. We doubt if it will be wise to have you as a friend." Lubdhak countered that if the crow can be your friend, why do you object to me. Mantharak asked, "Can fire and water, gods and demons, mongoose and snake be ever friends?"

The deer intervened and said, "Why argue about it? He only wants to be our friend. Let him be." But Hiranyak remained unconvinced and opined, "The fellow will destroy you by posing as a friend. We will have to be careful about him." Lubdhak was a cunning character. He gradually won their confidence. One day, he led Chitrang to a place where a hunter had laid a trap to ensnare some prey. The deer got entangled. He asked Lubdhak to cut the net and set him free. The jackal had other ideas. He saw the chance of savouring the meat of the deer. He came out with some excuse and said that he will do so in the morning. He thought that the hunter would kill the dear and skin him. He would then have the chance of eating some juicy meat with the bones. Chitrang realised that Lubdhak had tricked him and he was sure to die at the hands of the hunter. He rued the fact that he did not listen to his true friends and trusted this hypocrite and untrustworthy jackal. It was he who silenced his friends and forced them to allow this crafty jackal to stay with them.

As Chitrang did not return for a long time, the crow, the mouse and the tortoise grew anxious. They asked Laghupatnak to locate their friend. Laghupatnak found him entangled in the net and took Chitragreev and Mantharak to the site. They told Chitrang not to worry as they would leave no stone unturned to save him. Hiranyak unfolded the plan of his rescue. He said, "As soon as you see the hunter approaching, extend your stomach and hold your breath. Pretend that you are dead. The crow will sit on your head and peck at your eyes. I shall cut the net. The hunter would think that you are dead. At that time Mantharak would appear. The hunter would run after him to catch him. You speed away as soon as Laghupatnak gives you the signal."

As the hunter ran after the tortoise to catch him, Chitrang stood up and was gone in a few leaps. The hunter threw his stout staff at the deer which hit the jackal hiding in a bush. Mantharak quietly plunged into the pond. The jackal died then and there. The hunter went away greatly disappointed and the four friends returned to their abode. It is true that sincere friends are rare. The mean pose as friends and get you into trouble while a true friend will help you even at the cost of his own life.

❑ ❑ ❑

5. The Hermit and a Mouse

There was a Shiva temple in a big city in the south. A hermit named Tamrachurna lived in that temple. He eked out his living by begging alms. He kept the extra foodgrains in a vessel and hung it up on a nail on the wall. This extra good grains he distributed amongst the workers of the temple.

A mouse named Hiranyak also lived in a burrow in the temple compound with his family members. One day, his family members told him, "This *sannyasi* sleeps with the vessel hung up on the wall. It is difficult for us to reach it. You are strong and powerful. Why not try to reach the vessel? Then we will not have to run hither and thither for food." The mouse tried to reach the vessel and was successful in jumping into it. He then had his fill and threw the remainder to his family. This became a nightly routine. The hermit tried his best to save the foodgrains but the mouse managed to get at it.

One day the hermit found a way to scare the mouse. He brought a splintered bamboo and would strike it against the vessel. Being afraid of getting hurt the mouse kept away from the vessel and waited for an opportunity to get at the foodgrains. Many times the tussle between them went on for the whole night.

One day another sadhu, a friend of Tamrachurna, arrived at the temple. He had returned from a pilgrimage. Tamrachurna received him warmly. After dinner they lay down on matresses and started talking on matters of religion and morality. Tamrachurna's mind was on the vessel containing food and in between the talks he struck the bamboo at the vessel to keep the mouse off it. The other hermit whose name was Brihatsifak got annoyed at the attitude of his host. He thought that Tamrachurna was ignoring him.

He told Tamrachurna in an angry tone, "Tamrachurna, here I am talking to you but you are swinging that bamboo. I think I am not welcome here and should go elsewhere. It is written in the holy books that one should not stay at a place where one gets no importance or is ignored. It is said that one should leave even one's own father's house where there is someone who is short-tempered, jealous, arrogant, ignorant or foul-mouthed."

Tamrachurna replied politely, "Friend, a man in distress sometimes behaves contrary to his nature. I am not ignoring you. A mouse has made my life miserable. I am shaking the bamboo to scare him away." He then related that in spite of all his efforts the mouse was able to jump high and get at the foodgrains. It seemed that this mouse possessed some extraordinary powers.

Brihatsifak pondered for a while and said, "I feel this mouse has his burrow over some buried treasure. It is because of this that he is able to jump to such heights. You know, wealth intoxicates a lot. Even a mule starts behaving like a thorough bred horse under its influence."

Next day, both the hermits found out its burrow with the help of the footprints of the mouse. Then they went there with an axe and spade and dug out the place. They not only got hold of the stored foodgrains in the underground burrow but also laid hands on the buried treasure. In the process, good many mice got killed or injured.

Next day, when Hiranyak went to the temple, Tamrachurna again started banging the bamboo on the vessel. His friend told him not to do it any more. He said, "We have deprived the mouse of the strength. He will never be able to reach your foodgrains. You can sleep without any worry."

The mouse tried to jump into the vessel but failed. He tried his best but could not reach even half the height. It was only the heat of the wealth that enabled him to jump so high. Now he was helpless and his morale was shattered. His family and other dependants started ridiculing him instead of sympathising with his plight. They started leaving him one by one as he was unable to provide them food. Hiranyak was crestfallen at their selfishness and thought of leaving the place and eventually accompanied Laghupatnak to another place.

❏ ❏ ❏

Part-III

KAKOLUKIYAM

The third part of Panchatantra starts on the premise that one should never trust an enemy who comes to you posing as a friend. Given an opportunity and at an appropriate time, he may take revenge by plotting your destruction.

1. Why Crows and Owls are at Daggers Drawn

Meghvarna asked Sthirjeevi the reason for this enduring enmity between crows and owls. Sthirjeevi said that there was ample reason and told this story.

"Once all the feathered community gathered to discuss their problems. Swans, storks, cranes, *koels*, pigeons, roosters, parrots and all the species of birds

participated in this conference. The winged fraternity decided to elect their new king. Garuda, who carried Lord Vishnu on his back, was their king but they felt that he was neglecting his elementary duty of providing protection to them. He was so busy in serving the Lord that he did not find any time for redressal of their grievances. Bird catchers were spreading their nets everywhere and wantonly killing them. At this rate, they felt they were like a boat without a boatman on the high seas and so were destined to perish.

The swan said, "It is written in the holy books that a teacher who is unable to teach; a foolish priest; a ruler unconcerned with the plight of his subjects, arrogant friends and relations, a woman of loose morals and loud-mouthed friends usually destroy themselves. Hence, it is incumbent on us to elect a new ruler."

It was then unanimously decided to elect a new ruler who could look into their day to day problems. The stork suggested the name of the owl and the hawk seconded the choice. Nightly predators like bats also favoured the owl. Though many birds like swans and others had their misgivings, they could not gather enough courage to oppose the move and it was decided to make the owl the king of birds.

Hectic preparations started for the coronation ceremonies. Holy water was brought from all the rivers and centres of pilgrimages. Earthen pots full of water were kept at the site of coronation and brahmin priests were invited to recite from the *vedas*. A bird named Krikalika was anointed the queen. As the preparations were being made, a crow happened to pass that way. Seeing that preparations were on for some event, he stopped and enquired as to what was going on. He was told that the owl was being crowned as the new king of the birds. As a matter of fact, the birds were not happy to see a crow in their midst as it is well known that a barber amongst human beings, a jackal amongst animals and a crow amongst birds are wily, though clever creatures.

The crow had a hearty laugh on hearing this news. He said, "It is strange that you are making this day-blind bird of fearful appearance a ruler. You have here a plethora of good-looking, prudent, and learned birds like swans, peacocks, parrots, *koels* and storks in your midst. I see no wisdom in your decision."

The swan said that the owl was capable of protecting them. The crow replied, "One has to protect oneself first before protecting others. How can this king of fools protect you when he hides in some cave during the day and comes out only by night? The night creatures are generally predators or thieves."

The crow counselled, "We already have a valiant ruler in Garuda. He is the favourite of Lord Vishnu. Our enemies tremble in his presence. It is not necessary that he has to be present amongst us. The mere mention of his name strikes terror in the minds of the enemies. Then you have ignored the fact that your action might bring upon you the wrath of the mighty Garuda."

Hearing this the birds got panicky and started consulting one another regarding the next step. In the end they decided to postpone the coronation. The stork slipped away from the scene quietly followed by the hawk. Gradually everybody left. The owl was getting fidgety at this delay. He could not see that the place was totally deserted and also knew nothing about the interference of the crow resulting in the abandonment of his coronation. He asked Krikalika as to the reason for the delay. She related the story from the beginning to the end and blamed the crow for all that had happened.

The owl was beside itself with rage. He said, "I have done nothing against the crow. He has needlessly interfered and deprived me of the honour. He will now have to face the consequences of his uncalled for meddling. From now on each and every crow will be the enemy of our species. Let Garuda protect them if he can." So saying he flew to his abode.

Hearing this, the crow was in jitters. He thought to himself, "I have unnecessarily made this cruel and violent species the enemy of my people. I am supposed to be wise, but I forgot the golden rule that one should not publicly humiliate anyone. Now who will protect us from these predators who attack only during nights when we will be helpless. What could be done now? There is nothing now but to repent the unwise action for as they say a deed once done cannot be undone."

2. Meghvarna and Aridarman

Just outside the city of Mahilaropya in the southern region, there was a huge banyan tree in a forest. The tree had hundred roots. It sheltered a large number of crow families. Their chief, Meghvarna was a worried man. A little away from the tree, a large number of owls lived in a cave on a hill. Their chief was named Aridarman. Crows and owls are natural and eternal enemies. Aridarman came out of the cave when it was dark and would kill stray crows that he found and then hid in his cave. He had killed hundreds of crows.

Meghvarna was greatly distressed and did not know what to do. Aridarman attacked during the night when they were helpless. The number of crows was fast dwindling. One day, Meghvarna called his advisors to find some solution to this situation. He told them that the enemy was very clever. They did not know from where the owls came and after the attack disappeared in the dark. He told them that it was advisable not to allow the strength of the enemy or any sickness grow. They should be tackled as early as possible.

Meghvarna had five advisors. First, Ujjeevi spoke, "It is prudent not to fight a stronger enemy. It is better to strive for peace for war causes great loss and damage." After him the second advisor Sanjeevi opined, "One should never strive to buy peace with a ruthless enemy. Even then, the enemy will not hesitate to destroy us. Hot water will also extinguish the fire. We must strive to fight and defeat the enemy with all the resources at our command."

Meghvarna turned to the third advisor, Anujeevi, who said, "In my opinion, we should migrate to some other safer haven. Our enemy is powerful and cruel. If we stay here he is bound to finish us off one by one. We should then add to our strength and at an opportune time attack the enemy and gain victory over him." Prajeevi spoke after him. "In my opinion, none of the three courses suggested will work. We should stay here and battle them. One is always strong in his abode. A crocodile is able to bring the mighty elephant to his knees when he fights him in his own territory. We ought to strive to fortify this place and give them a fight."

Meghvarna turned to the third advisor, Anujeevi, who said, "I differ from all. We should try to find some powerful allies. We should strengthen ourselves by taking help from many quarters. You must have seen that an elephant can be bound by a rope made from weak strands."

After hearing all of them, Meghvarna called on the most experienced member of his family. He was old and wise. Meghvarna apprised Sthirjeevi of the situation they faced. Hearing all the details, Sthirjeevi said, "All your councillors have given their opinions according to their wisdom and capacity. They are right in many ways. In my opinion, the matter requires use of a fifth column. You should first have a peace treaty with your enemy. During peace, try to earn their confidence but never trust them. In the meantime, make full preparations for an all out war at an opportune time. You should employ some secret agents to find the weak spots in their defence through them. It is rightly said that these agents act as the eyes and ears of every ruler."

Sthirjeevi offered to go to the enemy camp to find out their strength and weakness. He said, "From today, you spread the word that we have fallen out. Start criticising me in harsh tones. Even arrange for a mock fight between us. Sprinkle some blood over me after the mock fight. Then leave me under this tree and migrate to some distant hill. Leave the rest to me. I shall try to make friends with Aridarman and find out all about his place. Then we can plan to destroy him with his clan."

Meghvarna did all this and abandoned the banyan tree with his entire clan. The secret agents of Aridarman informed him that Meghvarna has run away. Aridarman came to the banyan tree in the night and occupied it. Then they heard Sthirjeevi moaning under the tree. He was in a bad condition with blood all over his body. He asked the owls to take him to their chief as he had to tell him a lot of things. Aridarman himself arrived on the scene. Sthirjeevi told him in halting tones, "Meghvarna has done this to me. He wanted to attack you. I asked him to desist from this course. He got enraged and thought that I have joined your camp. Now I am at your mercy. I mean to help you in destroying Meghvarna who has treated me so cruelly."

Aridarman turned to his advisors before taking decision in the matter. A minister named Raktaksh said, "An enemy is always an enemy. We should not let him live." This was opposed by another minister, Kruraksh, who said, "It is against law to kill someone who has sought shelter with you. It would be something mean and base." Another minister, Deeptaksh said, "He is right. Many a time a person from the enemy's side proves a valuable ally. We can get a lot of useful information from him."

Two other ministers, Vakranas and Prakarkarn also opined that it was not proper to kill the wounded crow. Aridarman ordered that Sthirjeevi be carried to his abode and looked after well. Raktaksh was worried at this decision. He told Aridarman, "My lord, an enemy should be eliminated when he is weak. He may be wounded, weak and helpless but after all he is from the enemy camp. I think you have been taken in by his story. You might regret it one day."

Sthirjeevi became anxious. He felt that Raktaksh could demolish his well laid plans. He enacted another drama to impress Aridarman. He asked him to arrange for some firewood so that he could immolate himself. After all, his life was not worth living. The crows had thrown him out and then the owls doubted his intentions. This had the desired effect and Aridarman decided to give shelter to the wily crow.

Raktaksh assembled his family and followers and addressed them, "I think it is not advisable to continue to live with the foolish Aridarman and his followers. They are on the path of destruction. If the common people are fools, the rulers protect them. A foolish ruler is protected by the learned and wise. But where all the three are fools, one should leave that place at the earliest." Next day Raktaksh left. Sthirjeevi was highly relieved as he felt that the thorn in his flesh was removed at last.

Sthirjeevi started preparations for destroying the owls in right earnest. He thought that the best plan would be to set the cave of the owls on fire. He started collecting dry grass and firewood at the entrance of the cave. Everyday he went out to collect firewood and stocked it at the entrance of the cave. The owls thought that he was building a nest for himself. They had no inkling about his real intentions.

When he had collected sufficient firewood to set fire to the cave, he sent words to Meghvarna that he has made all arrangements to set the cave of the owls to fire. He asked him to bring lighted sticks for that purpose. As the owls were unable to see during the day, they were bound to die of suffocation inside the cave and if they tried to come out, they would be roasted by the fire. The crows could easily kill the day-blind owls.

Meghvarna arrived with his army of crows. The crows had lighted sticks in their beaks. They set fire to the dry grass and wood stacked at the entrance and all around the cave. A few owls who managed to come out were quickly liquidated by the hordes of crows. Most of them were either suffocated to death or roasted alive by the fire. Meghvarna returned to the banyan tree with the other crows. He praised Sthirjeevi for accomplishing the destruction of their enemies. He said, "You lived amongst them for a long time. Please tell us how you fared."

Sthirjeevi said, "It was nothing. Yes, I had to go through some difficulties but I suffered them gladly in the hope of future redemption. Living with enemies is like walking on a naked sword. You take one false step and you are finished. But I endured it all so we may have a peaceful future. As it was, the owls were simpletons. I have never seen such a foolish society anywhere. There was only one who doubted my intentions and left with his family. I am happy that I have succeeded in my mission."

❑ ❑ ❑

3. To Each His Own

The saint Yagyavalkya was head of an ashram situated on the banks of the river Ganga. Many other saints and monks lived in that *Ashram*. One day, Yagyavalkya was returning to his hermitage after his bath in the river. A female mouse fell from the sky right in front of him. It seemed that a hawk that was carrying it in his claws had dropped it. The saint felt pity on the helpless mouse. He put it on a large leaf. He sprinkled water from his *kamandal* on it and it turned into a girl. He returned to his hut with the girl in his arms.

He accosted his wife and said, "Good lady, we have no children of our own. Accept this girl as a daughter and bring her up." The wife took charge of the girl and lovingly brought her up as her own. As time passed, this girl reached the age of marriage. The wife drew the saint's attention to it and told him that as their daughter is now of marriageable age, a suitable match had to be found out.

The rishi agreed and said that he would find the most accomplished and suitable groom. If she is inclined I can ask even Sun god to accept her as his bride. He called Sun god who immediately presented himself before the saint. Yagyavalkya told him that the girl sitting beside him was his daughter and if she agreed, he desired him to marry her. Then he turned to his daughter and said, "Daughter, he is Sun god, a very suitable match for you. Would you like to marry him?"

The girl replied, "Father, he is very hot. I will feel very uncomfortable in his proximity. Please call some better groom." The *rishi* asked Sun god if there was anyone more powerful than him. The Sun god replied, "Yes sir, cloud is definitely more powerful than me. I become invisible when the cloud covers me."

The saint invoked the cloud to appear before him. As cloud appeared, he told his daughter that if she approved of him, she could be married to the mighty cloud. The daughter said, "He is so dark, please find someone better." The saint turned to the cloud and asked if there was anyone more powerful than him. The cloud said that air was stronger than him as it can easily scatter him.

Air was invoked and as he presented himself, the saint asked his daughter if she approved of god Pawan. The daughter observed, "Air is very fidgety. Will never stick to one place. How can I marry such a person?"

The Air god told the saint that the mountain was more powerful than him as he can always block his passage. The saint called upon the mountain to come forthwith. He presented himself and the saint asked his daughter if she approved of him as a husband. The girl thought for a while and said, "Oh father, he is so hard and stationary. Please find someone better." The saint enquired of the mountain if he could suggest someone better and stronger than him.

The mountain replied, "Though I am very powerful and can stop everything from passing through me, still I consider mice to be more powerful. They can cut through me and build their homes in my belly." The saint invoked the king of mice and asked his daughter if she approved of him as her bridegroom.

The girl was in raptures to see the Mouse king. She felt that he was the most suitable groom she could think of. She turned to the saint and said, "Father, turn me into a mouse again and let me marry this handsome mouse." It was an easy thing for the saint to do. He thought that one cannot forget one's origin and love for one's kind is natural.

❑ ❑ ❑

4. The Fools' Fraternity

Sindhuk, a bird, lived on a huge tree in a hilly region. Sindhuk was a remarkable bird. His droppings turned to gold. One day, a bird catcher went to the hills to catch some birds. As he passed that tree, he was amazed to see the droppings of a bird transform themselves into gold. The hunter had spent his entire life in entrapping birds but had never seen such a miraculous thing.

He laid his net under that tree, and sat at some distance. It was sheer coincidence that Sindhuk got caught in his net. The bird catcher was elated. He transferred the bird to a cage and returned to his house *post haste*. As he reached the house, he pondered over the matter. What could he do with the miracle bird? If anyone got scent of the bird and informed the king, he was bound to be hauled up. He decided that it was better to be on the right side of the ruler. He could get a nice reward from the king if he presented the bird to him.

The bird catcher proceeded towards the palace to present the bird to the ruler. The king was extremely pleased to have such a miraculous bird. He called his attendants and instructed them to look after the bird with care. A minister, who was with the king at that moment, told him, "Your Highness, you have believed in the words of an unreliable person like that bird catcher. How can you believe that the droppings of this bird turn into gold? No one has ever seen or heard of such a thing. I think it would be foolish to keep this bird. It is better to release it." The king immediately ordered its release.

Happy to be free, the bird flew to the main gate of the palace and sitting there thought to himself, "First, I was foolish to get caught into the net of the bird catcher. The bird catcher was a bigger fool to have presented me to the king for fear of punishment. The biggest fool amongst us was the king who released me on his stupid minister's advice. The minister had proved himself to be a great fool for tendering that advice without testing whether my droppings actually turned into gold. Really, we all belong to the fools' fraternity." Then he flew back to his perch on that tree.

❏ ❏ ❏

5. Names of the Powerful Carry Weight

Chaturdant, the elephant king, lived in some forest with his herd. As there were no rains for many years, all the sources of water had dried up. The animals and birds living in that area faced extreme shortage of water and food. The elephants approached their chief and pleaded, "Many of our people including small children are on the brink of death because of acute shortage of water and food. Many have died already. If we do not relocate to some other place, we all face extinction."

Chaturdant pondered over the problem and said, "I am reminded of a pond which is always full of water as it is connected to an underground source. Let us all shift to that place." The entire herd started for that pond. As it was very hot during the day, they travelled only in the night. It took them five nights to reach the new pond.

Their joy knew no bounds as they sighted the pond. They entered it eagerly and frolicked in it for the whole day. Then they came out to feed on the branches of the trees around the pond. Hundreds of rabbits lived in underground burrows with their families around the pond. As the elephants roamed about, their homes were destroyed. Not only that, many rabbits were crushed to death under the feet of elephants. Many others suffered grievous injuries too.

The rabbits got worried about the wanton destruction of their hearths and home. They gathered together to discuss the ways to save themselves from the marauding herd of elephants. They all agreed that the situation was grave. In view of the draught, it was certain that the elephants would stay out there for quite long. They would come daily to the pond to drink and bathe and trample many of them. In this way the entire population of rabbits would be decimated in no time.

An old and wise rabbit opined, "The best policy for us would be to abandon this place. We cannot fight the massive elephants. It is said one should abandon the village for saving the family. One should not hesitate to desert the world to save oneself from disaster."

Many rabbits opposed him saying, "We have been living here for generations. How can we leave it so abruptly? It would be better to find some way to scare the elephants into leaving this place." Hearing this a rabbit suggested, "Our king, Vijay Datt lives in the galaxy of moon. We should send a competent messenger to the king of elephants who can convince him that we are *chandravanshis* (descendants of moon) and our king Chandra Deo does not want them to stay here. Maybe, he can be duped to leave this place with his herd."

Another rabbit stood up to speak, "I think we can depute Lambkarn for this task. He is very clever and most suitable to be our diplomat." Everyone agreed with the choice. Lambkarn immediately left to see Chaturdant as a messenger of the Moon god. He went up a high hill and proclaimed loudly, "Listen, you good for nothing elephants. How dare you use this pond? Are you not aware that this pond belongs to the Moon god. It would be better for you to leave this place forthwith and never return to it."

Chaturdant got scared as he heard the name of Chandra Dev. Gathering courage he asked, "But, who are you?" Lambkarn, the rabbit, boldly replied, "My name is Lambkarn and I live in the galaxy of Moon. Shri Chandra Dev has sent me as his messenger." The chief of the elephants replied, "Chandra Dev is also our god. We cannot ignore his orders. You let me know his command." Lambkarn sensed his plan was succeeding. He said, "Yesterday, you have trampled to death many rabbits. Amongst them were many members of my family. The Moon god is greatly annoyed and has asked me to give this message. If you do not want to face his wrath, do not go to that pond again."

Chaturdant got a little suspicious and enquired, "But, where is Moon god?" Gathering his wits, Lambkarn immediately replied, "He is at present in the pond itself. He has come to console the families of rabbits whom you have so wantonly crushed to death." "If that is so, please take us to the pond. I would like to have his *darshan* and then, I promise, we shall leave this place."

Lambkarn asked him to come alone and took him to the pond. He showed Chaturdant the reflection of moon in the water and said, "See, the god himself is in the pond. Do not disturb him in any manner as he is meditating. He may be annoyed if he is disturbed. Pay your respects quietly and leave." Chaturdant bent on his knees and raised his trunk to salute the Moon god. He assured Lambkarn that he would never enter that pond and left with his entire herd. This story illustrates the reach and influence of the powerful. Mere mention of their name can bring about desired result in the same way as Lambkarn got rid of the elephants by mentioning the name of the Moon god.

❑ ❑ ❑

6. The Golden Swans

Chitrarath was the ruler of a kingdom. He had a pool in his palace which he named *Padmasar*. He had given shelter to a flock of golden hued swans in the pool. These swans shed a golden feather every six months which the ruler accepted in lieu of permission for use of the pool. As this arrangement was quite profitable for the ruler, he took good care of his guests. This arrangement of mutual benefit continued for a long time.

One day, a huge golden hued bird arrived at that pool. The swans objected to his stay in the pool. They told the newcomer that he could not stay there as they

had taken the pool on lease from the ruler and paid for their stay with golden feathers every six months. The giant bird was adamant. He said, "It is the duty of the ruler to treat everybody in the same manner. He cannot provide special privileges to some and deny the same to others." A dispute arose between them.

The giant bird went to meet the ruler. He first praised him to the skies and then related the dispute with the swans. He tried to vitiate the mind of the ruler by telling him that the swans did not respect him and did not care for his displeasure. The swans claimed that they had exclusive right to use the pool as they paid the ruler for its use with golden feathers. The ruler felt humiliated when the bird told him that the swans claimed that the ruler could do nothing to them.

Nobody likes to be talked about like this. The ruler was naturally enraged. In a fit of anger, he ordered his soldiers to kill all the swans. The leader of the swans sensed that something was amiss as he saw the armed soldiers approaching the pool. He asked his flock to fly away to some other place.

The ruler soon realised his mistake. The giant bird could not give him golden feathers. He thought to himself, "It was foolish of me to believe a stranger. Then without investigating the truth of the matter, I ordered the swans to be killed. The swans had taken shelter in my pool, and I tried to harm them. Now nothing can be done except to repent my foolish action."

❑ ❑ ❑

7. United, the Weak can Prevail

A very fierce snake named Atidarp lived in an underground burrow. One day he took a narrow path to come out of its hole. He suffered many injuries and blood oozed out of the wounds. As the ants smelled blood they gathered in large number to lick the blood of

the serpent's body. The snake tried his best to shake them off. The ants did not give up. They clinged to the snake. The snake was helpless before the horde of ants that attacked him. His wounds got worse and he died. This story illustrates the fact that if the weak get together, even a powerful person can be brought to his knees.

❑ ❑ ❑

8. Greed Never Pays

Hari Datt was a poor brahmin. He subsisted on the meagre income that he had from agriculture. His land holding was also small and as such he was always hard pressed. He also had a lot of spare time as his fields did not require much labour. One day, he was lying in the shade of a tree in his fields. He saw a cobra coiled up near a bush with his massive hood spread out. The brahmin thought that the snake could be the god and protector of that area. As he had never worshipped him, he never got good returns from his crops. He decided to placate the snake god.

The brahmin went to his house and brought milk in an earthen bowl. He placed it at the mouth of the burrow in which the snake lived and prayed, "Protector of this area! It was because of ignorance that I have not paid my respects to you. I have realised my folly. Please forgive me and accept this humble offering." Next day when he went to that spot he found that the milk had been taken and there was a gold coin in the earthen pot. Hari Datt was happy that the snake god had accepted his offering and given him a gold coin as token of his blessing.

From that day he made it a point to keep a bowl of milk for the snake at dusk. In the morning, he collected the gold coin. It so happened that he had to go to the neighbouring village for some work. He instructed his son to keep the bowl of milk for the snake god. The son did as desired by his father. Next day he found a gold coin in the empty bowl. That set him thinking. He thought that there would be a hoard of gold coins in the underground burrow of the snake. Why not dig it up and get hold of the entire wealth at one go. In the evening, he kept the bowl of milk at the mouth of the hole. The snake came out to drink it. The son gave a blow to the snake with a stout stick he carried. The snake was furious. He recoiled and bit the young man. The son died on the spot.

As the news of the death of the young man reached the village, his relatives arrived on the spot and cremated him. Next day, Hari Datt returned and was apprised of the sad news. He did not feel sorry for his son. He calmly said, "It had to happen. My son got his just punishment for his greed. Greed had blinded him so much that he tried to kill the snake who was our benefactor, guest as also family god. One who does not show mercy to someone who has taken refuge with you, usually ends up like this."

In the evening he took a bowl of milk to the snake. He apologised for the misconduct of his son and asked for forgiveness. The snake did not come out and said from inside his burrow, "You have come here because of your greed for gold coins. For that you have even forgotten that I am the killer of your son. Neither can you forget the loss of your son nor can I forget the injuries inflicted by your son. In the above circumstances, we cannot have cordial relations. You must know that once the bond of affection is broken, it cannot be cemented again by insincere protestations. I did not give you the gold coins in return for the milk that you offered me. I did it as I sensed that you had genuine respect for me. I helped you so that you could get rid of your grinding poverty. Please go away and never come here. I am giving you a last gift."

The snake came out with a precious necklace and placed it before Hari Datt and went back. Hari Datt picked up the necklace and proceeded towards his house ruing the greed of his son.

❑ ❑ ❑

9. Guest is God Incarnate

Once a cruel hunter lived in a forest. He traversed the forest continuously in search of birds of prey. His own relatives did not like his cruel ways and tried to make him see reason. They eventually abandoned him. The hunter built a hut for himself in the forest itself.

One day, in spite of his best efforts, he could not lay his hands on any bird. It was nearly dusk and he suffered from the pangs of hunger. He had no hopes of finding any prey but somehow a female pigeon got trapped in his net. He put her in a cage and started for his hut. Suddenly a storm arose and the entire forest was lashed by hailstones. He was deep inside the forest far away from his shelter. The cold winds made his life miserable. He was literally shivering. He searched for some big tree for taking shelter under it. He espied a big tree and stood under it.

Stricken with both cold and hunger, he prayed, "Residents of the tree, I have come to seek refuge with you. Cold and hunger have brought me to the brink of death. I pray to you all for succour and shall always remain grateful for any help." By coincidence, the mate of the female pigeon caught by him lived on the same tree. He was worried about the fate of his mate. As he saw his mate in the cage, he felt helpless as he could not do anything for his companion. He lamented, "Shame on my life that I cannot help you." The female pigeon consoled him and said, "My lord, one cannot erase destiny. This hunter has caught me as it was ordained. We all suffer pain or pleasure according to our deeds in previous life. At the moment, the hunter is your guest, please arrange for his food and save him from death. It is your prime duty."

The pigeon replied, "You are asking me to care for this cruel hunter who has caught you and would roast you for dinner as soon as he reaches his home." The female argued, "My lord, in this world, everyone behaves according to his inborn nature. Does it mean that we should forget our prime duty of entertaining a guest?"

The pigeon thought that she was right. He approached the hunter and asked what could he do to alleviate his suffering. The hunter said, "This extreme cold is killing me. Please arrange for some fire." The pigeon flew off and brought back dry leaves and twigs. He lighted the fire. The hunter warmed himself. Now the pigeon thought of feeding the hunter. He realised that he had no food to offer him. He pondered over the problem for some time as to how to feed the guest who had taken shelter at his place.

Then he approached the hunter and addressed him, "Revered guest, I have been unable to arrange for anything for you to eat. Unfortunate is the person who

cannot feed a guest. As such, I offer my body to you."
So saying he non-chalantly entered the fire. The hunter
was dumbfounded at this sacrifice of the pigeon. He felt
remorse and decided to give up his life of a hunter. He
rose and set the female pigeon free.

The female pigeon was broken-hearted and wailed
loudly, "My lord, you have done your duty. How can I
live without you?" She also jumped into the fire. The
hunter could not believe his eyes. He could not imagine
such a tragic result of his hunting activities. He broke his
bow and arrows and tore the net to smithereens. He
decided to atone for his sins. From then on, he moved
about the forest like a demented person. He renounced
the world and started living like a *sadhu* devoting his life
to the welfare of the birds and animals of the forest.

10. Beware of Enemy Within

People who are unable to keep their mutual secrets and spill them out usually become the cause of each other's destruction. It then becomes easy for others to target them and destroy them, as were the two serpents in this story.

A king named Dev Shakti ruled in a city. His son was in a distressing state. A serpent had entered his body and had made his stomach his home. Because of this the prince became weaker by the day. In spite of best medical aid there was no improvement in his health.

The prince himself was dejected and lost all hopes of a healthy life. Disgusted with his situation, he left his father's kingdom and started living in a far off kingdom. There he lived like a common beggar and slept in a temple during nights. He knew his days on earth were numbered. The name of the ruler of this kingdom was Bali. He had two young daughters. The princess came to see their father every morning to greet him. The elder princess always said, "Father, whatever I have in this world is due to you." The king was pleased and loved this daughter. The second princess said, "May god grant you the fruits of your deeds just as I enjoy them because of my deeds in previous life." The king was not happy to hear this. He thought that his second daughter did not give him any credit for all that she has got in life because of his bounty.

One day, as the second princess came to greet him in the morning, he lost his temper and decided to teach her a lesson. He called the minister and said, "Throw this princess out of the palace. Marry her to the first poor foreigner you find, so that she can reap the benefits that destiny has ordained for her."

The minister got the princess married to the prince with a snake in his stomach who was living in a temple in dire circumstances. The princess gladly accepted the prince as her husband taking it to be god's will. After marriage, they left for living in some other domain. In the new place, the princess chose a spot near a lake. Leaving a bodyguard to look after the prince, she went to the nearby market to purchase the daily requirements with the other servants.

On return, she was amazed to see that the snake that lived in the stomach of the prince was peeping out of his mouth and airing himself. The prince was soundly sleeping with his head near the burrow of another snake, who was also out of his hole. Though scared, the princess hid behind a tree as it seemed that the snakes were talking to each other.

The second snake spoke to the snake who lived in the prince's body, "You mean fellow, are you not ashamed of your actions? Why are you wasting the life of this handsome prince by making your home in his body?"

The snake who lived inside the prince's body retorted, "Get rid of this holier than thou attitude. Aren't you sitting pretty over two vessels full of gold coins in your hole?"

The arguments between them warmed up as they looked towards each other with blood red eyes. The snake from the hole said, "If only someone knew that if the prince is given *kanji* laced with black pepper in hot water, you would be dead in no time." It was then the turn of the first snake to reveal the secrets of the second snake. He said, "You can also die if one was to pour hot water mixed with oil into your hole." In this way, both revealed the secret of their own extermination.

The princess, who was listening to these dialogues from behind the tree, did not lose any time. She boiled water and mixed it with hot oil and poured it in the hole of the snake. Then she mixed *kanji* with black pepper and gave it to her husband to drink. Her husband regained health in no time. She dug out the pots full of gold coins with the help of her servants.

Then she returned to her father's place. This time the parents received her with warmth and affection. She lived happily thereafter with the husband secure in the belief that one gets what is ordained for him or her because of good or bad deeds of previous life.

11. When Thieves Fall Out

Drona, an extremely poor brahmin, lived in some city. Begging for alms was his only source of livelihood. He never had enough clothes to save him from the rigours of winter nor enough food to keep his body and soul together. Seeing his dire plight, a rich benefactor gifted him two male calves. The brahmin somehow managed to feed the calves. They turned out to be healthy and strong.

The brahmin planned to sell them for good price. It would have been of some help in relieving him of his grinding poverty. As luck would have it, a thief saw those calves. He decided to steal them before the brahmin disposed them of. One night, he started for the village of the brahmin for that purpose.

As he reached the outskirts of the village, he came across a person of fearful countenance. His eyes were red like burning coals. His large teeth protruding out of his mouth scared the thief. Gathering courage, the thief asked that dreadful person of his identity. The man replied, "I am Satyabachan, a demon on prowl. But who are you?" The thief answered timidly, "I am Krurverma. I am going to this village to steal the calves of Drona, the brahmin."

The demon replied, "I shall accompany you to the house of the brahmin. I have not eaten for many days. While you steal the calves, I shall make a meal of that brahmin. Let us go together." As they reached the house of Drona, they hid in a dark corner and waited for the opportune time when they could accomplish and carry out their nefarious designs.

The brahmin was in deep slumber. The demon made a move towards him to devour him. The thief stopped him in his tracks and said, "Do not be so impatient. First, let me take away the calves. Then you can satisfy your hunger." The demon countered, "If the calves make a sound, the brahmin may wake up. I would then be nowhere. So allow me to kill the brahmin and then you can take away the calves."

The thief did not agree. He said, "Suppose you are not able to kill the brahmin as he gets up. I would not be able to steal the calves. So let me do my work."

The dispute could not be settled amicably. Tempers rose and with that the decibel level of their shouting at each other. The brahmin got up at the commotion and sat in the bed. The thief approached him and said, "This demon intends to make a meal of you." How could the demon lag behind? He stepped forward and said, "This fellow also has evil intentions. He came here to steal your calves."

The brahmin did not hesitate for a minute to make his move. He got hold of a thick staff and pounced on both and gave them a good thrashing. The demon and the thief made a quick exit to save their lives. The brahmin sat thinking to himself. Sometimes your enemies also do a good turn when they fall out. Their quarrel proved a boon to me. I am spared both my life and my calves.

❑ ❑ ❑

12. Justice of the Vile

A partridge named Kapinjal lived in a hollow of a tree. The partridge left his nest in the morning to search for food. One day, Kapinjal left with his friends for a rice field. He did not return in the evening as was his wont. Then he went missing for many days and the other birds living on the tree got worried. Kapinjal might have fallen prey to some hunter or a wily cat.

During one night, a rabbit named Sheeghragati arrived and finding the hollow vacant, made it his home. Surprisingly, Kapinjal came back after some days. He looked healthy and well fed. He must have fed on the freshly ripe milky rice grains. As he saw the rabbit in his home, he lost his temper and shouted at him, "How dare you occupy my home. It will be better for you to vacate it forthwith."

The rabbit was adamant. He replied, "How is this your home? It might have been in the past but as I found it vacant, I have occupied it. Hence, it is mine now." They argued for some time. The rabbit then suggested that they can place the dispute before some arbitrator for decision.

As they were getting ready to find some impartial arbitrator, a cat heard all that passed between them. The wily cat saw an opportunity of making a meal of both of them. The cat proceeded towards the river bank. He had string of beads in one hand and stood on one leg. He made a pretense of worshipping Sun god and muttered to himself, "This world is a mirage. Everything in this world has to come to an end. There is only one way to obtain *nirvana* (salvation), that is, path of right conduct."

The rabbit heard all this and suggested to Kapinjal, "The cat seems to be a learned person well versed in the scriptures. We make him the arbitrator in our dispute." The partridge was naturally scared of approaching the cat but eventually agreed to the rabbit's suggestion. He asked the cat to settle their dispute hinting that he could feed on the guilty party.

At this suggestion, the cat opened his eyes and said, "How dare you make such an ignoble suggestion? I have renounced the world as well as all violent ways. I now subsist on fruits and vegetables. I am quite old and have become hard of hearing. You need not be afraid of anything. Please come closer and state your cases."

The rabbit and the partridge moved forward to tell him about the dispute. As they got near, the cat pounced on them like a flash of lightning and killed them.

The moral of the story is that never go to your natural enemy for settling your disputes and do not believe his words if he assures you that he has turned a new leaf. You may have a tragic end like that of the rabbit and the partridge.

❑ ❑ ❑

13. Brahmin and Three Thugs

A brahmin named Mitra Sharma lived in some place. He had many rich clients for performing religious ceremonies. He went to one such disciple in another village and told him, "I need a goat to perform a *yagya* next month. Can you give me one?" The disciple immediately arranged for a healthy goat. Mitra Sharma started for his village. The way to his village lay through deserted area and dense forests.

As he was in a hurry to cross the forested area as quickly as possible, he lifted the goat to his shoulders and walked briskly. He had fear from wild animals that lived in that forest. Three thugs saw him with the goat on his shoulders. Their mouth watered to see the healthy goat. They immediately decided to get hold of the goat by hook or crook.

One of them disguised himself as a traveller and sat under a tree as if he was taking rest. As Mitra Sharma passed his way, he said, "Panditji, what has come over you? You are carrying this dog on your shoulder. You are a brahmin and should know about *dharma* better. Shame on you." The brahmin angrily replied, "Have you eyes? You are calling a goat a dog." "Do not get angry," replied the thug, "it is none of my business if you carry a dog on your shoulders. I only intervened as you are a brahmin. You must be knowing that a dog, a rooster and a *chandal* (one who skins dead animals) are declared to be untouchables."

The brahmin shrugged his shoulders and went his way doubting the sanity of that man. A little further the second thug met the brahmin. He also called the goat a dog and asked the brahmin to cast it away. It was against religion, he opined. The brahmin scolded him in angry tones and asked him to mind his own business. The thug went away and the brahmin moved forward towards his village.

He had only gone a little further that the third trickster met him. He asked the brahmin as to why he was behaving in this irreligious manner, who had heard of a brahmin carrying a dog on his shoulders. The brahmin was now in doubt. Not one but three total strangers had called the goat as dog. As he thought deeper, doubts regarding the thing that he was carrying took roots. He was convinced that he was carrying a dog. He threw the goat on the ground and hurried towards his village. The thugs were happy to carry away the goat.

Such are the ways of the world. Even learned people can be easily deceived by frauds for it is well known that if a lie is repeated continuously, it can pass off as truth.

❏ ❏ ❏

14. The Speaking Cave

A lion named Kharnakh lived in some forest. He could not find any prey in spite of best efforts during the day. It was nearly time of sunset that he came across a cave. He entered it thinking that some animal should be living in it. Its resident would return to it during night. Then he could kill it and satisfy his hunger.

The cave belonged to a jackal named Dadhipuchh. He returned in the night. As he approached the entrance, he saw paw marks of a lion going into it. There were no corresponding marks to indicate that the lion had come out of it. He pondered over the matter and decided to make sure if the lion was still inside.

After thinking a while, he hit upon a plan. He stood at the entrance of the cave and shouted, "Cave, O' Cave". Naturally the cave remained silent. The jackal again said, "Cave, have you forgotten the agreement that we made. You are supposed to reply when I accost you on return. It is alright if you do not wish to welcome me tonight. I shall seek shelter elsewhere." Then he stood silently at the entrance.

The lion thought that the cave must have been welcoming him everyday. Today it is silent because of my presence. It would be better that I respond, otherwise the jackal would go away. He is bound to treat my response as that of the cave. The lion roared loudly. His roar caused a panic as small animals started running to find some shelter.

The jackal's suspicion that a lion was inside the cave was confirmed. He laughed and commented, "It is the first time that I have heard of a speaking cave." He left the place thinking that his clever strategy succeeded in fooling the lion. The foolish lion fell into trap. It never occurred to him that caves do not respond or talk.

❑ ❑ ❑

15. The Clever Snake

A snake named Mandvish lived in a hilly region. He had become old and could not easily find a prey. He struck upon a plan by which he could easily find prey without much effort. He went to a pool full of frogs. There he sat on a rock with a drawn face. Seeing him sitting with such a sad face, a frog asked him, "Uncle, what is the matter with you? You seem to be glum. You are not even trying to find some food for yourself."

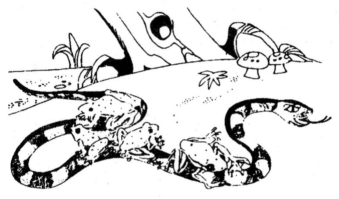

The snake replied, "I have no desire to eat today. In the morning, I followed a frog near a pond. Some brahmins were reciting holy books on its bank. The frog hid himself amongst the brahmins. I could not sight the frog and by mistake bit a son of the brahmin. His mother was inconsolable at her son's death. She cursed me, 'You have killed my innocent son. You will have to atone for it by acting as a carrier of frogs on your back. So I am here to carry you on my back'."

The frog dived in the pool and spread the story. The king of the frogs came out and sat on the hood of the snake. As he was not harmed, others took courage and sat on the body of the snake. Mandvish took these frogs round the pool. The frogs and their king enjoyed the ride.

Next day, Mandvish reached the pool to give ride to the frogs. He moved very slowly. Jalpad, the king of frogs, asked him the reason for the slow speed. The snake replied, "I have not eaten so I am feeling weak. I can hardly move." Jalpad told him, "If that is the matter, you have my permission to eat a few frogs from this pool."

Mandvish got what he desired. From that day, he got his food without making any efforts. The foolish frog king did not realise that he was instrumental in liquidating his own people for the pleasure of having a ride on the back of the snake. Another snake, who saw Mandvish carrying frogs on his back, reprimanded him reminding him that he was playing with his natural food. Mandvish replied, "Friend, you will not understand it. In this way, I get my food without any efforts." In this clever way, Mandvish made a meal of all the frogs of that pool, without any of them getting wise to his clever strategy.

❏ ❏ ❏

Part-IV

LABDHAPRANASH

Labdhapranash means that you lose what you had gained. **Acharya Vishnu Sharma** *told the princes that one who does not lose one's composure and retains one's mental keenness, comes out with flying colours at times of distress and danger.*

1. The Clever Monkey

A monkey named Raktamukh lived on a big Jamun tree near the sea. This tree bore delicious fruits all the year round. One day, a crocodile named Karalmukh came out of the sea and sat under the tree to bask in the sun. The monkey was eating the fruits of the tree at that time. As he saw the crocodile, he addressed him, "Friend, you are my guest at the moment. Our holy scriptures have prescribed that a guest should be treated as God incarnate. Please accept these fruits." So saying, the monkey offered him the choicest *jamuns* to Karalmukh. The crocodile liked the taste of the sweet heavenly fruits. He talked to the monkey till the evening and then returned to his abode.

Next day, the crocodile again came out to meet the monkey. They talked about many things and a deep friendship developed between them. It then became a daily routine for the crocodile to come and talk to his friend. Karalmukh ate the fruits to his heart's content and took some for his wife when he went home in the evening.

The crocodile's wife also found the fruits delicious. One day she asked her mate, "From where do you get these delicious fruits?" The crocodile related the story of his friendship with Raktamukh who not only fed him with these fruits, but also insisted that he carry some for his mate. The crocodile's wife then said, "The monkey eats these sweet fruits every day. I think his heart should be as tasty as these fruits. You will have to bring his heart for me to eat. I feel I shall attain eternal youth if I partake of it."

The crocodile reprimanded her for such evil thoughts. He said, "He is my friend and I have accepted him as my brother. Can I betray a brother? You better get rid of such mean desires." But the female crocodile did not let the matter end so easily. She countered, "The monkey lives on land and you are a water creature. Howcome he has become your brother?" The crocodile tried to reason with her. He told her, "In this world, there are two types of brothers. One type is that takes birth from your mother's womb. The other type is whom you accept as your brother. The latter is considered superior to the former as the relationship is based on mutual trust and affection."

It is well known that the female of every species is generally successful in bringing her male round to her point of view. It is difficult to make them see reason once they decide to get a thing. The crocodile explained that it was impossible to kill the monkey and get his heart as he lived on a tree while he stayed on the ground. He could not climb a tree. The wife remained unconvinced and used her last weapon to bring him round. She gave him an ultimatum, "If you fail to bring the monkey's heart for me to eat, I would go on hunger strike till death." This put the crocodile in a dilemma as he loved his wife dearly. Next day, he went to see his friend with a heavy heart.

Raktamukh sensed that his friend was sad. He asked, "You seem to be worried. Is everything all right with you?" Karalmukh who had made up his mind to surrender to his consort's desire replied, "Friend, it is a small matter. Today I had had a fight with your sister-in-law. She accused me of being ungrateful. She told me that I should have invited you to my home as you have been so kind in giving us such mouth-watering fruits. She has said that she would not eat or drink anything till she has entertained you at our home."

The monkey replied, "I would love to be your guest. But, I can only walk on land while your home is in the sea. How can I accompany you to your home?" The crocodile replied, "That is no problem. I live on an island. You can ride on my back." Raktamukh did not doubt anything, as trust is the foundation of friendship. Without trust and friendship, relations and affection cannot take roots. The monkey jumped on the back of his friend and the crocodile swam towards his home.

As the island was not visible for miles around, the monkey asked, "Friend, how far is your island?" The crocodile thought to himself that the monkey was now helpless in mid sea and there was no harm in telling him the truth. He said, "To tell you the truth, I have brought you to kill you. My wife is adamant that she should have your heart to eat. She thinks it should taste quite delicious."

The monkey got the shock of his life. He realised that he had been tricked by the ungrateful crocodile. But he did not lose his cool. He smiled and said, "Why did you not tell me earlier? It is a small matter. My heart is lying in the hollow of the tree. If you had told me at the beach, I would have given it then and there. Please take me back and I would hand it over to you. I cannot even think of disappointing your gracious wife."

The foolish crocodile felt elated. He said, "Let us hurry back. You can hand me over your heart." He turned back and brought the monkey to the beach. Raktamukh jumped out and climbed the tree. The crocodile waited under the tree. As time passed and the monkey did not come down with the heart, he said, "Why this delay my friend? Please come down with the heart so that I can take it to my wife. She must be anxiously waiting for it."

The monkey laughed and replied, "You are a fool. Nobody has two hearts in his body. You have betrayed the trust of a friend for which there is no atonement. I was a fool to have trusted you. It is said that one should never trust an unreliable person and even a reliable one should not be trusted implicitly. Now go away and never come to me again!"

The crocodile realised that the clever monkey had tricked him. It was stupid of him to divulge the truth to the monkey in mid sea. He decided to make another effort. He said, "I was just joking my friend. My wife looks upon you as a brother. She has cooked a lot of things for you. Please come with me as she would be sorely disappointed otherwise."

The monkey replied, "Once bitten twice shy. You cannot deceive me twice. The wise have said that one should never trust a hungry person and the vile have no sense of mercy. One can gain lost wealth, prestige and reputation but trust once betrayed can never be regained. Go away and never come back." The crocodile returned to his place regretting that he succumbed to his wife's desires and lost a good friend in the bargain.

❏ ❏ ❏

2. Never Invite an Enemy to Settle Your Feud

Gangdatt was the chief of a family of frogs that lived in a well. Though he was wise and learned, the other frogs were always looking for an excuse to humiliate him. As they did not see eye to eye with him, there were many quarrels. Because of these insults and fights, Gangdatt was very miserable and did not know what to do.

One day, in an angry mood, he came out of the well. As the well was fitted with a Persian wheel for drawing water, he jumped into one of the water cans and came up. As he reached the outside world, he pondered over his plight. He wanted to take revenge on his relations who had made his life so miserable. Suddenly, he espied a black cobra entering his hole. Gangdatt thought of taking his help in liquidating his opponents. It is laid down that a strong tormentor can be set right by a stronger antagonist. A thorn can always be taken out with another thorn.

Having reached this decision, Gangdatt reached the hole of Priyadarshan, the snake, and called out for him. The snake was astonished at the strange voice that was calling him. Hence he took the precaution of answering from inside the hole and asked as to who was calling him. Gangdatt revealed his identity and also told him that he wanted to make the snake his friend. Hearing this the snake came out and said, "It is strange that you want to be my friend. Nature has ordained that you are my food. Can fire and grass ever be friends? If the hunter befriends the hunted, he will go hungry."

Gangdatt admitted that Priyadarshan was right, and said, "I have come for your help as I have been tormented by my enemies. It is said that one should take help of even an enemy to liquidate one's own enemies." Then he related the story of his differences with the other frogs living in the well. He offered to take the snake to the well where he could get his food easily by preying on the frogs that he would point out as his adversaries. Priyadarshan had become old. As it was, he found it difficult to hunt frogs or other prey due to his old age. He saw in this a golden opportunity to get his food with ease.

But the snake had one problem. He told Gangdatt that the snakes did not have feet to walk. How would he enter the well? Gangdatt assured him that it was no problem. He knew a secret passage to the well. Then there was also a hollow spot at the edge of the water level which he could use to live. The snake agreed to follow him. Gangdatt asked him to promise that he would make a meal of only those frogs that he would identify. He would not cast his evil eyes on his family. Priyadarshan readily agreed.

Gangdatt's wife remonstrated that in spite of his being so wise, how could he take this foolish step to invite a snake into their home! She opined that he had invited the destruction of his entire clan. Gangdatt assured her that the snake would leave after annihilating his enemies. For Priyadarshan, it was the best period of his life. He made a meal of all the frogs shown by Gangdatt.

As all the enemies had been eaten up, Gangdatt approached the snake to leave the well and go home. The snake had got used to easy life and replied, "Where can I go now? My house must have been occupied by some other snake. This is my home now. It is for you to provide me with food. If you fail to do so I will have no other option but to feed on your family." Gangdatt was scared. He regretted that he brought the snake to his home. If he angered him, he was bound to prey on his family and wipe them off. It is truly said that friendship should always be between people of same status and strength. Making friends with stronger person is like taking poison with your own hands.

Priyadarshan started making a meal of the members of Gangdatt's family one by one. He did not even spare his wife and one day swallowed his eldest son Yamunadatt. Tears welled into his eyes. But nothing could be done now. He himself had invited disaster. He should have thought earlier that if he planned destruction of his own people, he himself was bound to be destroyed one day.

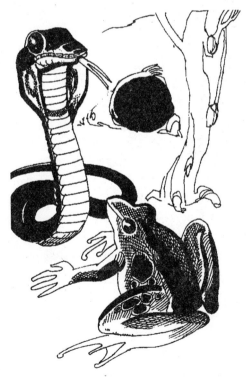

He thought of escaping from the well. But it was risky as the snake lived near the Persian wheel through which he could hope to escape. It was sheer luck that Priyadarshan himself provided him an opportunity to escape. One day, he told Gangdatt, "Friend, I am very hungry. There is nothing to eat here. Please arrange for some food." Gangdatt saw this opportunity and said, "You need not worry. If the frogs of this well are finished, I can bring many from other nearby wells." Saying this he jumped into a container of the Persian wheel and rode it to the top of the well. He heaved a sigh of relief at having escaped from the clutches of Priyadarshan.

Priyadarshan got worried when Gangdatt failed to return. He was also very hungry and had nothing to eat.

He approached a monitor lizard living in the well, "Sister, please search for Gangdatt. Many days have passed since he went out. If you find him, ask him to return. Tell him that as I have accepted him, as a friend, I cannot think of harming him. If he has not been able to persuade frogs to come here, he need not worry. I am feeling so lonely without him."

The monitor lizard searched out Gangdatt and delivered the message of the snake. She said, "Your friend is feeling miserable without you." Gangdatt replied, "Please tell him that I have no intention of returning to that well. Have you not heard the saying, 'once bitten twice shy'. A hungry person can commit any sin. One should not trust a hungry person. He has proved to be vile as well as he broke his promise." So saying, Gangdatt walked away.

❑ ❑ ❑

3. The Story of a Foolish Donkey

A lion named Karalkesar lived in some forest. Dhusarak, a jackal, lived with him and looked after his needs. One day, Karalkesar was involved in a fierce fight with a rogue elephant and was grievously injured. Many of his bones were broken as the elephant caught him and hurled him on the ground. It became difficult for him to move about. Unable to hunt, the lion and the jackal faced starvation. As the pangs of hunger became unbearable, the lion asked the jackal to bring some animal to his place whom he could easily kill.

Searching for some prey, the jackal reached the outskirts of a village. There he found Lambkarn, a donkey, grazing on the river bank. The jackal approached the donkey and addressing him as maternal uncle, said, "Seeing you after a long time. You are looking very feeble." The donkey replied, "What can I say? My master, the washerman, is a very cruel man. He puts heavy loads on me but never cares to feed me properly. He only gives me a small quantity of dry grass that is hardly sufficient."

The jackal grasped the opportunity and sympathising with him, offered, "If that is the matter, you can come with me. I will take you to my place where it is green all around. There is a pool of sweet water in the vicinity. You can graze to you heart's content and roam about in the forest. In no time you will be healthy and strong." The donkey objected, "It is all right but I am a domesticated village animal. The forest is full of wild animals who would kill me in no time." The jackal said,

"Do not worry on that count. Nobody will dare to harm you. My word is law there. I have liberated many donkeys from the tyranny of their masters including three young female donkeys. You can be very happy in their company."

The donkey was taken in by the sweet talks of the jackal and started for the forest. The jackal took him to the place where the hungry lion was waiting to pounce on him. As Lambkarn reached the bushes, Karalkesar gave him a blow with his paw. Somehow Lambkarn avoided it and escaped for his life. The jackal was angry and told the lion that he had become useless for all purposes. He could not even kill a donkey and let him escape. The lion was crestfallen and requested him to try and bring some other animal. Dhusarak said that he would try again to bring back the same donkey. The lion expressed his doubts if the donkey could be persuaded to come back. The jackal reassured him and said that he should see to it that he did not fail to kill him this time.

The jackal again went to the village and met the donkey. Lambkarn was furious. He said with sarcasm in his tone, "Welcome my nephew, you really took me to

a nice place. If I had not been alert, I would have been dead. What was that animal who attacked me? He had a powerful paw." Dhusarak laughed and said, "Uncle, you are the limit, you did not even recognise the female donkey that rose to receive you. You just got scared and ran away." Lambkarn was doubtful and remarked that the animal was too large to be a donkey. The jackal said, "She lives in a healthy atmosphere and naturally was stronger than you city bred animals. She has asked me to bring you as she wants you to be her mate."

The foolish donkey accompanied the jackal. This time the lion did not falter and killed him in one stroke. The lion asked the jackal to guard the body as he went to take bath. The jackal being very hungry ate the ears and heart of the donkey. The lion was furious and asked the jackal as to how he dared to eat before him. The jackal told him, "You are getting angry for nothing. If the donkey had ears and heart, could he be lured again after having seen you once." The lion was satisfied with the explanation and they both sat down to eat. As for the donkey, he paid with his life for repeating his mistake. Anyone who does not learn from his mistakes, ends up like Lambkarn, the foolish donkey.

❏ ❏ ❏

4. Neither Here Nor There

A farmer couple lived in a village. The farmer was of advanced age but the wife was much younger than him. She was not happy with her life. A trickster sensed that he could take advantage of the situation. Once, when she came out of her house, he approached her and said, "My wife is dead and you are not happy with your husband. Why not elope with me. We can live together." The woman was more than happy at the suggestion. She replied, "I do not mind. First let me get hold of money and valuables from my house. My husband has lot of money but never puts it to any use. It will come handy to make our life comfortable."

The thug asked her to meet him at the same spot early next morning. During the night, the woman collected all the money and valuables on which she could lay her hands and tied it in a bundle. She met the trickster at the appointed place and they went in the direction of south. As they travelled for some time, the thug thought to himself, "Is there any sense in wasting my life with this middle-aged woman. I should try to get hold of her money and valuables and desert her. With the money, I can get settled with a younger and more charming wife. Then, suppose her husband comes following her, it will be another problem."

Soon they came upon a river. The trickster decided on a plan of action to get rid of the woman. He told her, "This river is very deep. It will be difficult to cross it with you and your heavy bundle. I think it will be better to take the bundle first and then I can return to take you across." The woman readily agreed and gave him the bundle containing money and other valuables.

The thug took charge of the bundle and then said, "It will be difficult to cross the river with your heavy clothes and jewellery. I think you better hand over the clothes and jewellery that you have on your person." The unsuspecting woman handed him her clothes and jewellery as well. The thug swam to the other bank with everything and left the woman on this side of the river. A lot of time passed but the man did not return. He never had the intention to do so.

The woman waited for him anxiously. She saw a female jackal pass by with a piece of meat in her mouth. At the same time, a fish came to the bank. The female jackal put the piece of meat on the ground and plunged to catch the fish. The fish quickly dived into the water. In the meantime, a hawk swooped down from the skies and took away the piece of meat lying on the ground.

The farmer's wife laughed at the female jackal and made fun of her for having lost both the fish and the piece of meat. The female jackal retorted, "Why are you laughing at me when you are a bigger sucker than me? You left your husband and your lover has forsaken you. He has also taken all the money and valuables you stole from your husband. Now what are you waiting for in this naked state? He is not going to come back to you. Haven't you heard the saying that a bird in hand is better than two in the bush." So saying, the female jackal went away leaving the woman to rue her stupidity.

❑ ❑ ❑

5. The Clever Jackal

A jackal named Mahachaturak lived in some forest. He came upon the body of an elephant during his wanderings in the forest. He was very happy that he could eat for days. He went round the body and tried to cut open the skin to feed on the flesh. But the skin of an elephant is very tough and his teeth were not sharp enough to cut it open. He wondered how to get over the problem. Jackals are wily and clever creatures.

A lion passed that way and Mahachaturak hit upon a plan to eat the flesh of the elephant. He went to the lion and paid his respects. Then he said, "Lord of the jungle, I am your obedient servant. I have been guarding the body of the elephant for you. Please feed on him." The lion looked at him with disdain and said, "You should be aware of the fact that lions do not feed on prey that they have not killed themselves. Only the scavengers of the forest like jackals and hyenas do so." The lion moved away.

The jackal was happy that the lion did not accept his invitation. Soon a tiger passed that way. The jackal thought, "I have got rid of one but now comes another intruder." He thought for a while and said to the tiger, "Uncle, why have you come here to court disaster. This elephant has been killed by a lion who has asked me to keep guard on the body. He has gone to the river for his bath. He has asked me to inform him if a tiger comes this way as he has to settle scores with him for having fed on his prey sometime back. So please make a move." Hearing this the tiger lost no time in leaving the place.

A leopard arrived at the spot. The jackal thought that he could be used to cut open the skin of the dead elephant as leopards have very sharp teeth. He approached the leopard and pleaded, "Dear nephew, seeing you after a long time. You seem to be hungry. This elephant has been killed by a lion and is under my protection. Why not have a bite or two?" The leopard hesitated to feed on a lion's killing, being scared of lion's fury. The jackal reassured him, "Do not worry. Eat without fear. As soon as I see the lion approaching, I shall warn you."

The leopard agreed to eat and as he tore open the skin to start eating, the jackal warned, "Nephew, the lion is approaching. Run for your life." The leopard slunk away. As the leopard had already made a hole in the body of the elephant, the jackal merrily started feeding on it. The flesh lasted for many days.

❑ ❑ ❑

6. The Stupid Donkey

A washerman named Shudhhpat lived in a city. He had a donkey. Due to paucity of good grass, the donkey had become very weak. The washerman did not know what to do. One day, the washerman came across the dead body of a tiger. He skinned the tiger and brought the tiger skin to his house. He thought of a plan to feed his donkey. He covered the donkey with the tiger skin and left him in the fields to feed on fresh

vegetables and crops. Every night he did it and brought back the donkey at dawn. In no time, the donkey became strong and healthy.

The villagers thought that a tiger was on prowl and did not dare to go to their fields during the night. One night as the donkey was peacefully grazing in the moonlit night, he heard another donkey braying in the distance. The donkey could not resist and started braying in unison. As the villagers heard him braying, they realised that a trick had been played on them. They came to the field with stout staffs in their hands and started thrashing the poor donkey. The donkey fell down and died. The washerman who thought himself to be very clever lost his only means of transport.

7. Slaves of Their Wives

King Nand was ruler of vast domains. His empire extended upto the seas. He was brave and learned. His minister, Varruchi was also versed in scriptures and statecraft. Both were highly respected by the common people for their qualities.

One day, the queen of Nand got annoyed with him for some reason. Nand tried all means to please her but she remained adamant. Nand loved his wife and could

not bear to see her unhappy. He asked her what would make her happy again. The queen replied, "If you really care for me, then walk round this room on all fours with me astride. You will also have to neigh like a horse." Nand had no other option but to abjectly surrender to his wife's whims. Varruchi's secret agents apprised him of this incident as to how the king crawled on all fours and neighed like a horse.

It so happened that the minister's wife also got annoyed with her husband. He asked her as to what he should do to make her happy. She asked him to get his head shaved if he wanted her to be happy. Varruchi obliged her.

Next day, when Varruchi reached the court, the king asked him jestingly, "Was there some special festival on which you got your head shaved." Varruchi replied in the same vein, "Yes, your highness, you should know it. It was the same festival on which even a brave and proud ruler has to neigh like a horse and carry his wife around the room on all fours." Nand hung his head in shame. He thought, "How helpless are men before the whims of their wives that they have to behave like fools. Truly, women can tread on the self-respect of men whenever they desire."

❏ ❏ ❏

8. Inborn Nature Cannot be Changed

A lion couple lived in a forest. The lioness had given birth to two male cubs. As she was unable to hunt, the lion brought her some prey. One day, in spite of his best efforts, he could not find any. In the evening, he found a jackal cub. Picking him up in his mouth, he brought him to his cave and said, "I could get nothing except this cub. I did not kill him as it is said that one should never kill a learned person, a woman or

a child. If you so desire, you can kill him and satisfy your hunger." The lioness replied, "How can you expect a mother to kill an innocent cub. I shall bring him up as my third son."

The jackal cub also grew up with the two lion cubs feeding on the milk of the lioness. He roamed about the forest in their company quite oblivious of his identity. One day, the three cubs came across an elephant in the forest. The lion cubs got ready to attack the elephant. The jackal cub asked them to desist and said, "It would not be wise to fight him as he is very powerful. I suggest that we run away from this place." Saying this he ran for their abode. The lion cubs also got demoralised and followed suit.

When they reached their abode, the lion cubs told their mother about the cowardly behaviour of the jackal cub. They made fun of him. The jackal cub lost his temper at being called a coward. He remonstrated and abused the lion cubs. He even got ready to fight with them and teach them a lesson for their insolent behaviour. The lioness intervened and told the jackal cub to calm down. She told them that a fight between brothers is like inviting destruction of the family.

But the jackal cub was still beside himself with rage. He claimed that he saved the lion cubs from danger and they had the temerity to call him a coward. The lioness took him aside and said, "I have to tell you something. Though brought up on my milk, you are not a lion but a jackal. Upbringing and company do not change inherent nature and instincts. You are safe till my sons do not discover about your real identity. I think you better leave now. There are chances that my cubs become cowards in your company." The jackal shivered as he heard this from his foster mother. He quietly left the place and started living with his own people.

❑ ❑ ❑

9. The Unfaithful Wife

A brahmin lived in some city. His wife was a very quarrelsome woman who did not see eye to eye with his relations. She had daily fights with them even on trivial matters. The brahmin loved his wife but was sick of these daily hassles. He decided to settle in some other place and left his native place with his wife.

The journey was long. As they reached a forest, the wife felt thirsty and asked her husband to arrange for some water. The brahmin went in search of water which he found at some distance. He was shocked to find his wife lying dead when he returned with the water. He sat dejected near the dead body and wailed loudly at his misfortune. Suddenly he heard a voice from the skies, "If you want your wife to be restored to·life, you have to pledge her half of your remaining life."

The brahmin was more than glad to do it. He immediately gifted half of his life to his dead wife. She rose up as if nothing had happened to her. Happily they resumed their journey. Soon they reached the outskirts of a city. They found a beautifully laid garden there in which flowers of different varieties were in full bloom. The brahmin asked his wife to stay in the garden and left for the city to buy some eatables. A lame man was singing there while working on the Persian wheel. He had a melodious voice. The brahmin's wife got enamoured of the lame man. She went to him and expressed her love for the singer. The lame man readily agreed to her proposal of love. She asked him to accompany her, which was also accepted by the grateful singer. In the meantime, the brahmin returned from the market.

As they ate, the wife suggested, "The lame man at the well is also hungry. Let us give him some food." The husband provided the lame man with some food. Again the wife told her husband, "When you leave me alone, I feel scared. We should take along this man. He can keep me company as also do odd jobs." The brahmin did not like the idea. He said, "As it is, we are finding it difficult to manage our affairs. This fellow will be more or less hindrance. How can we ferry him on our shoulder?" The wife was determined to take the lame person. She replied, "It will not be your problem. I will place him in a basket and take him on my head."

The brahmin agreed reluctantly and the lame man became their companion. Once the brahmin lay down for rest on the boundary wall of a well and went to sleep. The woman who had become besotted of the lame man, saw her chance and pushed her husband into the well. The lame man asked her as to why she had done this. The woman replied that she did not want him to come between her and her new found love. Then she

collected all the things and placing the lame person in the basket, left for the city.

The guards of the city got suspicious when they saw her roaming in the city with a man being carried in a basket on her head. They took both of them to the ruler. She told the ruler, "Sir, this lame man is my husband. Our relations have misappropriated all our property and turned us out of our house. I have come to this city so that I can do some work and eke out a living."

The ruler felt pity for he thought that a hapless woman had been wronged by her people. He accepted her as an adopted sister and also granted her the income of two villages so that they could live comfortably. By sheer coincidence, her husband also reached that city after wandering at many places. He had been rescued from the well by some traveller. The unfaithful wife was scared to see him in the city. She immediately rushed to the ruler and said, "Brother, a brahmin, who is antagonistic to my husband, has come here. He may murder my husband."

The ruler believed the story and ordered the brahmin to be arrested. The brahmin was taken to the ruler for punishment. The brahmin told him, "You have a fair reputation and are supposed to be just. This woman has taken away something from me. Please have her return it to me. Then you can punish me as you like. I will accept it."

The ruler turned to the woman and asked if she had taken anything from the brahmin. She vehemently protested that she had ever taken anything from that man. The brahmin intervened, "If she thinks so, let her repeat these words. 'I give you back what you had given me.' I will be 'satisfied'."

The woman was nervous but had no option but to repeat the above words. As soon as she uttered these words, she fell dead. The ruler was surprised at the turn of the events. He asked the brahmin to explain. The brahmin related the entire story in detail. The ruler released the brahmin and sentenced the lame man to be blinded. He observed, "Frailty is part of a woman's character and like goddess of wealth, she cannot stick to one man."

Part-V

APARIKSHIT KARAK

One should never attempt a thing without gaining full knowledge about it and without thinking about its consequences. Before coming to any conclusion, all aspects should be gone into, otherwise the end result will be disastrous.

1. Greed is Unmitigable Evil

Four brahmin youths lived in some city. They were fast friends but all of them were extremely poor. They were very miserable on this count. It is true that poor are neglected by their friends, relations and the world at large. They decided to try their luck in some foreign land and thought of moving to Avantika, famed for its wealth.

The city of Avantika is situated on the bank of river Kshipra. The four friends had their bath in the holy river and proceeded to the temple of Mahakaleshwar for offering puja. As they came out of the temple, they chanced to come upon the renowned *yogi* Bhairavanand. Bhairavanand had long, matted hair and was supposed to possess supernatural powers on account of life dedicated to *sadhna*. The four youth followed the savant to his *ashrama*. The *yogi* enquired from them the reason of their coming to Avantika. They replied, "We have come here to earn money and have vowed not to return to our native place till we become rich. We feel death preferable to poverty."

Bhairavanand replied, "Money and wealth are dependent on god's will." They countered, "We admit that a man can come into wealth if it is ordained. But, the courageous can change their destiny by efforts. You possess extraordinary powers and we seek your blessings and help." The yogi was pleased at their determination and firm resolve. He decided to help them. He gave each of them a lamp and said, "Proceed towards the Himalayas with the lamp in your hands. On the way, if the wick of your lamp falls to the ground, stop there and dig into the earth. You shall find hidden treasure. Take it and return. Do not proceed further if your wick falls." The four brahmin youths left on way to the Himalayas with the lamps in their hands.

After some days, the wick of the lamp of one of the youths fell to the ground. He started digging at that spot and found a copper mine. He told his friends, "Friends, let us take all the copper and return." The other three did not agree and said, "Do not be a fool. What will we do with this copper. We shall proceed further." The youth replied that he was happy with the copper and collecting it returned.

The three friends resumed their journey. After some time, the wick of the lamp of another youth fell on the ground. As they dug at that place, they found a silver mine. He asked his friends to collect the silver and return. The other two youths replied, "First it was copper and now silver. We may get gold after that. Why should we be content with silver if gold lies ahead?" The second youth loaded the silver on horses and returned content that he found silver.

Further ahead, the wick of another youth fell on the ground. They found a gold mine at the spot. He told his friend, "Gold is precious. Let us dig all of it and return." The fourth youth replied, "I am not such a fool. Haven't you marked that we got copper, then silver and now gold. May be a mine of precious gems lies ahead. Let us go further. Why settle for gold if you can get precious gems and stones." The third youth told him to go ahead and he would wait for him there.

The fourth youth went ahead with great expectations. The way was tortuous but he continued to press forward. His clothes got torn and blood oozed out of his feet. He was also very thirsty. He wandered about in search of water. Soon he found a man sitting at a spot. He had blood all over his body. A wheel circled over his head. The brahmin youth enquired from the man, "Who are you and why are you sitting at this desolate spot. I am very thirsty. Can I get some water nearby. Above all, why are you sitting under this revolving wheel?"

He had hardly completed his sentence when the wheel moved over to his head. The brahmin youth was surprised and asked the man, "What is the meaning of this? How has the wheel come over my head?" The man replied that it had come over his head in identical circumstances. The brahmin youth enquired as to when and how it would leave him. The man replied, "It will leave you when some greedy person comes here and

asks you the same questions that you asked me. Then it would move over to the head of the enquirer."

The brahmin youth asked, "How long have you been sitting here?" The man put a counter question, "Who is the ruler these days?" The youth replied that it was the reign of King Veenavatsaraj. The man then replied, "I have lost all sense of time. I came here during the reign of Raja Ram. I came here in search of wealth with the lamp and found a man sitting here with a revolving wheel over his head. As I asked him about his plight, the wheel came over my head."

The brahmin youth expressed surprise at his surviving for such a long time without food and water. The man enlightened him, "This wheel is meant for extra greedy persons. When it revolves over your head, you neither feel hungry nor thirsty. Age and death do not affect you. It causes unbearable pain." Saying this the man hurriedly left the place.

The third youth who had got gold and was now free from all desires of more wealth, waited for a long time for his friend to return. In the end, he started in search of his friend. He managed to reach the spot where he found his friend sitting under a revolving wheel and covered with blood. He was pained to find his friend in such straits. The fourth youth told him, "This is the wheel of destiny." Then he related his sad story from beginning to end. The third youth told him, "Friend, I dissuaded you from going any further. In your greed, you did not heed my advice. Your greed for riches blanked out your sense of reason. Being a brahmin, you inherited learning and social status. But you lacked commonsense to differentiate between good and evil. Greed is a bottomless vessel. It can never be filled. Our sages have opined that prudence and commonsense are superior to book learning." He then took leave of his friend and returned to his native place. ❏ ❏ ❏

2. Seek Advice from the Wise

Mantharak, a weaver by profession, lived in some city. He worked very hard and even then could barely arrange for two square meals for himself and his wife. One day, his loom and other implements broke down as he was weaving some cloth. To make a new loom, he needed wood. He picked up an axe and went to a nearby forest to get wood. He selected a *sheesham* tree and climbed it to cut a few branches. A *yaksha* had his abode on that tree. As the weaver raised his axe, the *yaksha* appeared before him and pleaded,

"Please do not cut this tree. I live on it. You must be knowing that those who deprive others of their belongings, never prosper."

The weaver replied, "I am helpless. My loom and other implements are broken and I have to make new ones. I am a poor weaver and if I do not work daily, my wife and I shall go hungry. You can shift to some other tree. I need sturdy *sheesham* wood." The *yaksha* said, "I can understand your position. If you do not cut down this tree, I am willing to grant you a boon."

The weaver thought for a moment and said, "If that is so, let me go home and seek advice from my wife and friends as to what should I ask you for." The weaver climbed down the tree and proceeded towards his village. On the way, he came across a friend who was a barber by profession. He related the entire story to the barber and sought his opinion as to what he should ask as boon from the *yaksha*. The barber replied, "This is a lifetime opportunity for you. Ask him for a kingdom. You can be its ruler and live in pomp. You can appoint me as your minister."

The weaver told him that he would now seek the advice of his wife. The barber warned him against it and said, "It is not proper to involve women in this. The holy books prescribe that women should not be consulted on such matters. After all they are only interested in their creature comforts. That is why wise men have opined that those who go by their women's advice, suffer humiliation and problems. It is said that only in the house of a fool, wicked person, and a gambler woman have upper hand and that house generally suffers destruction, for women have a limited outlook."

The weaver remained unconvinced. He said, "My wife has stood beside me through thick and thin. She is a pious woman and I must consult her." He proceeded to his house and related to his wife the entire story of his encounter with the *yaksha* and his promise of a boon. He also told her that his barber friend wants him to ask for a kingdom. The wife vehemently opposed it. She said, "How much brain a barber can have; what does he know about governance of a kingdom. Uneasy lies the head that wears a crown. Then there are continuous conflicts, conspiracies and intrigues that worry a ruler. Of what use is a kingdom if you cannot even sleep peacefully?"

The weaver agreed with his wife and said, "You are absolutely right. Even great kings like Rama and Nala faced so many problems. Now tell me what should I ask as a boon from the *yaksha*." The weaver's wife thought for a moment and said, "With whatever you weave in a day, we meet our daily expenses. You ask the *yaksha* to give you another head and another pair of hands. You will then produce twice the amount of cloth and we can live more comfortably."

The weaver went back to the tree and approached the *yaksha*. He asked him to provide him with an extra head and another pair of hands. "So be it," said the *yaksha* and the weaver had two heads and four hands. He returned to the village in a happy mood thinking about his upcoming prosperity. As soon as he entered the village, the people thought of him to be a demon who had come to terrorise them. They came out with sticks and beat him to death. The weaver paid with his life because of the wrong advice of his wife who lacked knowledge of worldly affairs and practical things.

❑ ❑ ❑

3. Book Learning is Not Enough

Four brahmin youths lived in some city. They were fast friends. They decided to shift to some *gurukul* in the state of Kanyakubj to study under capable teachers. They studied the holy scriptures and became well versed in all branches of learning. After studying for twelve years they sought the permission of their teachers to return home. Though they had attained knowledge, they lacked everyday commonsense and were totally ignorant of worldly wisdom. Anyway, with their teachers' blessings they started back for their native place. As they were returning after twelve long years, they had forgotten the way to their native place. They reached a crossing where four roads converged. They stood perplexed as to which road would lead them to their place. As they stood there arguing about the road to take, a funeral procession passed that way. Many *mahajans* (traders or prosperous persons) followed the funeral procession. One of the brahmin youths remembered to have read in his book that one should follow the road taken by *mahajans*. The four decided to follow them.

The funeral procession stopped at the cremation grounds. Now again, they were at a loss as to which direction to take. They sat huddled thinking about the problem. They espied a donkey at the cremation grounds. Another brahmin youth opened his book and said, "It is written here that one should accept anyone as his kin whom he meets at some function or in the way, in tragic circumstances, during famine, if cornered by enemy, in royal court and cremation grounds." They immediately accepted the donkey as their relation and started showing their affection for the donkey and wiped its feet.

At the same time, they saw a camel running past them. They wondered what it could be. Having lived a cloistered life for twelve years, they were quite oblivious of worldly things. The third youth opened his book and said, "I know, this thing is *dharma*. Dharma travels very fast and this thing is also running fast." The fourth opined that they should unite *dharma* with their new found friend or relation. They dragged the donkey towards the camel and tied them together. The donkey belonged to a washerman. As he learnt of the foolish action of the youths, he came with a stick to beat them up. The brahmin youths made a quick exit to avoid being beaten up.

They resumed their journey and came to the bank of a river. They saw a leaf of the *palash* tree flowing in the river. One of them said, "I have read in my book that this leaf can be used to cross the river. It will take

us to the other bank." He jumped into the river to catch hold of the leaf. Soon he found himself in deep waters and shouted for help. Another youth entered the river to save him. He somehow got hold of the drowning youth's long tuft of hair. He remembered to have read in his book that if you see the whole being destroyed, save half of it and let go the other half. He took out a knife and severed the neck of his friend and saved it and let go the body. Now they were three of them and they resumed their journey towards their home.

As they moved forward, they reached a village. Seeing that they were learned brahmins returning from their schooling, the villagers thought of entertaining them. They received them warmly and three villagers invited one each brahmin to take rest and food at their homes. The host of one of the youths served vermicelli cooked in milk and sugar. As he sat to eat, he remembered to have read in the books that one who eats long things is destroyed. He refused to eat it.

The host of the second youth served him *chapatis*. He also remembered to have read in the books that spherical things diminish your life. He also got up and refused to eat the food served. The third brahmin was served *vadas*. There was a hole in the centre of *vadas*. He immediately remembered that anything with a hole in the centre brings misfortune. He did not eat the *vadas* and left. As such, all the three remained hungry. As the villagers learnt of their foolishness, they gathered and made fun of them. The brahmin youths left the village in a hurry to avoid further humiliation and ridicule. This story illustrates that it is not enough to have bookish knowledge. It has to be supplemented with worldly wisdom.

❏ ❏ ❏

4. The Foolish Barber

Manibhadra, a prosperous businessman, lived in the city of Patliputra. He was also a very generous person. He lavishly donated money to social and religious charities. Actually, he did it so recklessly that his financial condition became very insecure. He became very poor and this worried him a lot. He knew that living in poverty was a painful affair. With his money gone, there was gradual deterioration in the level of respect and adoration that he once enjoyed. After all, this world is so money-minded that for the poor, life can only be like living in hell. He did not know what to do. He made strenuous efforts to regain his lost status and money but luck did not favour him. In the end, he decided to commit suicide as life was no longer worth living without money and respect in society.

Having made this decision, he went to sleep. During the night, Lord Padmanabh himself appeared in his dream and spoke to him, "Give up the idea of ending your life. You have utilised your wealth in good deeds and have earned merit. I am pleased with you. In the morning, I shall come to your door in the guise of a monk. You hit me at the head. My body will then turn into gold. This gold will end your poverty and you can start afresh and live happily thereafter."

As he woke up in the morning, Manibhadra pondered over the dream. Will the dream come true? He thought that dreams were dreams and have no relation with realities of life. His mind was beset with doubts. His barber arrived to give him a shave. At that very moment, a monk, exactly like the one who had appeared in his dream, came to the door and asked for alms. Manibhadra was elated and hit him on the head with a stout staff. The monk fell dead on the ground and became a life size gold statue. He took it inside. As the barber had witnessed the whole affair, he made him promise not to breathe a word about what he had seen. He also gave him a lot of gifts to keep him in a happy frame of mind.

The barber promised to keep silent about the episode. At the same time, he was happy that he now knew how to get rich. He decided to try the experiment himself. If one monk can become gold when struck on the head, it was reasonable to believe that others could

also be transformed into gold the same way. He decided to invite many jain monks to his house and kill them. He would then be the richest person of Patliputra. Thinking about his future riches, he went to sleep.

Early morning he went to a big monastery of jain monks. He went to the head monk and fell at his feet. The head monk blessed him and enquired about the reason of his visit. The barber said, "I have come to invite you all to take food at my house." The head monk replied, "What are you talking about? We do not go out to the house of devotees like brahmins. At stipulated time, we go out to beg for food. We take only that much which is essential for living and nothing more." The barber was disappointed but made another effort. He said, "My lord, I am fully conversant with the ways of jain monks. My purpose is to present you with some valuable writing material and cloth for binding books that I have collected. I also intend to give some money for writing books. Please come and accept them."

The head monk accepted the invitation. The barber reached the monastery before the monks came out to beg for food. He requested the monks to follow him to his house. Expecting to get money and cloth, they readily agreed to accompany him. The barber invited them into the house and bolted the main door. He took hold of a staff and started belabouring them. Many died on the spot and others were grievously injured and wailed for help. Their cries attracted attention of the soldiers posted in the street. They entered the house and found blood all over the place. Those of the monks who could talk told them the story of the barber's butchery.

The barber was arrested and presented before the ruler for trial. The ruler asked the barber, "What made you kill these innocent monks?" The barber related what he had seen at Manibhadra's house and how he was tempted to repeat it and become rich. He was convinced that if one monk could become gold at the Seth's house, the other would also be transformed into gold.

Unconvinced at the fantastic story of the barber, the ruler called Manibhadra. Manibhadra related the story of his dream and how a monk came to his door next morning. He admitted that he killed the monk who turned into gold after death. The ruler held the barber guilty of brutally killing monks and sentenced him to death. He called the barber an impudent man and a diabolic killer who acted like this without thinking of consequences of his deed. The barber came to a conclusion without analysing all facts and acted in haste.

❑ ❑ ❑

5. Travel With Some Company

Brahmdatt, a brahmin, lived in a village. He received a message from another village to reach there. He informed his mother that he had to go on a journey. His mother advised, "It is always better to travel with someone. One should not embark on a journey alone." The son replied, "Do not worry. I am quite familiar with the way. There is no danger in travelling alone. I will have no problems."

The mother remained unconvinced. She went to a nearby pond and got a crab. She handed over the crab to her son and asked him to keep the crab as a companion for the journey. The brahmin kept the crab in a box of camphor in his bag and started for the village.

As the sun rose, it became very hot to travel. The brahmin lay down under the shade of a big tree to rest. He fell asleep. A snake, which lived in the hollow of that tree, smelled the camphor in the bag and came out. He tore open the bag to reach the box of camphor. As the box of camphor opened, the crab came out and encircled the neck of the snake in its pincer like legs. The snake tried its best to shake off the crab but the crab did not let go. The snake died as its neck was cut.

As the brahmin woke up he found a dead cobra lying near him. The camphor box was also lying open. He realised that the crab had saved his life. He thought about his mother's advice to have a companion during travel. She was right. He would have been dead if the crab was not with him. He started on his journey thinking that even a weak and insignificant companion can prove helpful during journey.

❏ ❏ ❏

6. The Musician Donkey

A donkey named Udhhat lived in some city. During the day he carried loads for his master. After taking work from him during the day, the washerman did not tie him up. The donkey was free to roam during the night. At day-break, the donkey presented himself before the master for work. This arrangement suited both the donkey and the washerman.

The donkey became friend with a jackal. They would gain entry into the fields and feed on tender cucumbers. In the morning, they parted and went their respective ways. The owner of the field in which they fed themselves did not know how to prevent them from entering his

fields. The donkey was adept in breaking the low level bond that he erected all around his field.

It was a moonlit night. Cool breeze was blowing. The donkey got into a romantic mood and said to the jackal, "Nephew, it is such a pleasant night. I feel like singing. Tell me what would you like to hear. I am well versed in classical music." The jackal got nervous and replied, "Uncle, you have forgotten that we are stealing food here. It is said that thieves should never give themselves away. Your voice is so harsh that it is bound to awaken the owner of the field. Why invite trouble? Eat your fill of these delicious cucumbers and banish all thoughts of singing in moonlight."

The donkey took umbrage at these words and replied angrily, "What do you mean? You know nothing about fine arts. I have memorised and practised all the classical *ragas*." The jackal apologised for his comments, but knew fully well that the donkey was bound to get them into trouble. So he told the donkey that he would like to listen to his song from a distance as it would be more enjoyable that way.

Saying this the jackal went out of the field and sat at a safe distance. The donkey started braying on a high note. The owner got up and rushed to his field with a stout staff in his hands. He got enraged to see the damage to his field and fell upon the donkey and thrashed him mercilessly. After some time, the donkey limped out of the field. The jackal met him and said, "I think you have been amply rewarded for your singing capabilities. I warned you but you did not listen to me. I knew you were in for trouble." The donkey, who was in great pains, said, "The fools are not expected to appreciate finer things of life. The buffalo would be indifferent to violin being played before her. In any case, that rustic has broken my bones instead of appreciating my fine signing." Then he limped away to his master's place.

7. Act in Haste, Repent at Leisure

Dev Sharma, a brahmin lived in some city. He eked out his living on alms. A female mongoose gave birth to a son. The same day the wife of the brahmin also gave birth to a son. Unfortunately, the female mongoose died after the delivery. Dev Sharma's wife took pity on the mongoose infant and took it under her protection. She brought it up as her son. The mongoose and human child grew up together under the loving care of the kind-hearted brahmin lady. They developed a deep bond of affection and the mongoose always

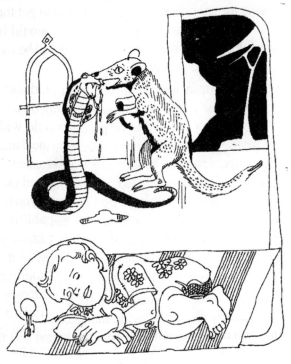

remained near the son of the brahmin. The brahmin lady was happy to see that they liked each other and generally played together as kins. The brahmin lady had some doubts about the safety of her child. She thought that an animal is after all an animal and cannot be implicitly trusted. It can some day harm her child.

One day, the brahmin lady approached her husband and told him, "I am going to fetch water from the well. You look after our son in my absence." By sheer coincidence, a man arrived to invite the brahmin to his house to receive alms. The brahmin left the house leaving his son in the care of the mongoose whom he considered to be his foster son. The brahmin lady got busy in gossip and did not return for some time. It so happened that a black cobra entered the house as soon as the brahmin left. The cobra advanced towards the cot of the child. The mongoose was sitting nearby watching over him. As soon as the mongoose saw the cobra, it attacked it. The enmity between mongoose and snake is well known. A fierce fight ensued between them and the mongoose was able to kill the snake.

As the brahmin lady returned to the house, the mongoose rushed to the door to welcome her. He was also excited as he expected to be praised for his brave deed of saving the child from the deadly snake. As the brahmin lady saw his blood smeared mouth, she exclaimed, "He has done it. This monster has killed my son." She was beside with rage and hit the mongoose with the water-filled pot. For a second, the mongoose looked at her with piteous eyes not understanding why the loving foster mother had hit him and then died.

The brahmin lady rushed inside the house. She found her son sleeping soundly and a dead snake near his cot. She immediately realised that the mongoose had saved her son from certain death. She beat her breast and fell on the ground wailing that she had killed the innocent mongoose without finding out the truth. As the brahmin returned to the house, she asked him to kill her as she was guilty of killing her innocent foster child. "I am a murderer," she wept. The brahmin consoled her and said, "Whoever reaches some conclusion without verifying facts, has to face agonising moments. Do not waste your tears. You should have first verified the truth. Now you have to repent your action taken in haste. There is nothing you can do except to bear it with fortitude and learn a lesson for the future."

❑ ❑ ❑

8. A Monkey's Revenge

Chandrabhupati was the ruler of some kingdom. He had many sons. The princes liked playing with monkeys. The king invited a group of monkeys to stay in the palace under his protection. Ushnas, the leader of these monkeys, was not only wise but was also well versed in ethics. The king looked after these monkeys with care. The princes had also kept many rams on which they used to ride.

These rams were a mischievous lot. Some of them would enter the kitchen and eat anything that they could lay their hands on. The cook was greatly annoyed and would hit them with anything he found handy. It could be a stick or any metal utensil. This tussle was a daily routine. Ushnas was greatly worried on this count. He told his flock, "This daily tug of war between the cook and the rams may prove disastrous for us. Suppose some day the angry cook throws up a lighted stick at them and their wool catches fire. The rams may enter the stable and set it on fire. The horses may get scalded. *Vaidyas* would be called to treat the horses. They are bound to ask for monkeys' fat which is prescribed in *Ayurveda* as ointment for burns. The king will not hesitate for a moment in killing us to save his horses."

The younger amongst the monkeys made fun of old Ushnas. They said, "You seem to have reached the age of senility. The king is fond of us. He treats us like his sons. It will be foolish to forsake the comforts of the palace in fear of some future danger." Ushnas made another effort to make them see reason and leave the palace. He said, "The book of wisdom says that one should abandon a place where there is friction. I advise that we move to some forest." Eventually, Ushnas left the palace for the forest as others refused to listen to his sage advice.

One day, it happened. Ushnas' fears came true. The cook threw a ligthed stick from the oven at the rams. The wool on their back caught fire. The nervous rams entered the stable and set fire to the grass stacked there. The fire spread and many horses suffered burn injuries before they could be taken out of the stable. The physicians demanded monkey's fat to treat the horses and the king ordered the killing of all the monkeys.

Ushnas heard the news in the forest. He felt miserable at this wanton killing of his people. He decided to take revenge. He wandered about in the forest thinking of ways to take revenge. Feeling thirsty he reached a pond to drink water. Being wise and cautious, he examined the outskirts of the pond before entering it to drink water. He found a lot of footprints of human beings and animals going to the pond, but there were no corresponding footprints to indicate their return. He decided not to enter the pond.

The pond was full of lotus flowers. The wise monkey picked up a hollow stem of a lotus flower and used it as a straw to drink water from the pond without entering it. Soon a ferocious demon came out of the pond and said, "You seem to be an intelligent person. How clever of you to drink water without entering the pond. I am happy with you and can fulfil any of your desires. This is my pond and anyone who enters it becomes my food."

The monkey thought for a while and asked, "How many men can you eat?" "Tens of thousands if they enter the pond. Outside the pond, I cannot harm anyone," the demon replied. The monkey told him, "I have to settle a score with a ruler. I can make him enter the pond with his entire family and courtiers, provided you give me the gem-studded necklace that you are wearing." The demon was more than happy to hand over the necklace to Ushnas.

Ushnas went back to the city of Chandrabhupati and roamed about the city wearing the costly necklace. Many enquired from him as to how and from where he got that invaluable necklace. He spread the story that he got it from a nearby pond. Whoever takes bath in that pond before dawn, gets a necklace like this.

The news about the miraculous pond spread and soon reached the ears of the king. He called the monkey to the palace and asked him if the news about the pond was true. The monkey answered, "This necklace that I am wearing is evidence that what I have told the people is true." The king expressed sorrow for his conduct at having ordered the killing of the monkeys. Ushnas replied that he was happy that they were of some use to their ruler. He offered to show the pond to anyone deputed by the king.

The king said, "There is no need to send anybody. I shall accompany you with my family to take bath in the pond and get as many necklaces as possible." The next day the king with his entire family and selected courtiers started for the pond accompanied by Ushnas, the monkey. They reached the pond before dawn. Ushnas told the king, "My lord, the necklaces are given if you take your bath at dawn. I suggest everybody enter the pond now and you wait for some time as I shall take you to a special spot where you will receive invaluable treasure." The king asked his family and courtiers to get into the pond. The demon was happy to make a meal of all of them.

As nobody came out of the pond for some time, the king got worried and asked the monkey the reason for delay. Ushnas climbed the tallest tree in the vicinity and said, "Listen you ungrateful ruler, the demon of the pool has devoured all those who entered the pond. You destroyed my family and in revenge, I have got your family killed. As you had brought me up, I have spared you as it is prohibited to kill anyone who has brought one up. You betrayed the trust of my family members who were under your protection. Today nemesis has caught with you."

The ruler was inconsolable at the death of his entire family, "How would I bear this tragedy?" he wailed. The monkey replied, "In the same way, as I have to bear the loss of my family at your hand. From now on, every moment of your life will be agonising and unbearable and you would pray for death as it would be more welcome than life itself."

9. The Learned Fools

Four sons of a brahmin lived in some city. The three elder brothers had acquired immense knowledge having studied under capable teachers. In spite of their learning, they lacked intelligence and everyday commonsense. The youngest brother had not studied the scriptures but was clever and possessed robust commonsense. One day, they discussed amongst themselves that though they have ample accomplishments to their credit, they still lived a life of want. They thought that of what use was their learning if they cannot use it for earning wealth and gaining recognition. A poor man, in spite of his learning, has no respect in society. They decided to go to the capital of that kingdom, where they hoped to earn merit and wealth.

The four brothers embarked on their journey. After a day's journey, they stayed at a place for rest. The eldest amongst them opined, "Our youngest brother is neither educated nor has he acquired any skill. He is intelligent but cannot earn any money. I think he should not accompany us and return from here." The second brother supported the eldest brother and asked the youngest brother to go home. The third brother did not like the idea. He said, "Subuddhi is our youngest brother. We have all grown up together. We have shared everything since childhood. We should not be so petty-minded. We should be large-hearted and should not entertain such thoughts for one who is youngest amongst us. I think he should also come with us."

It was then decided that the youngest brother would accompany them. As they proceeded, they came across a dense forest. As it was getting dark, they decided to stay under a tree. They found a stack of bones. The eldest brother opined that the bones seem to be of some wild animal. He said, "It is a golden opportunity to test our skills. The other two brothers agreed with their eldest brother. The youngest, Subuddhi, said nothing as the brothers prepared to demonstrate their skills.

The eldest brother got up and arranged the bones to give it the shape of a skeleton. The second brother did not lag behind and gave the skeleton flesh, muscles and blood. It now seemed to be a dead lion. The third brother knew how to put life into dead bodies. He got up to put life in the dead body. Subuddhi stopped him

and said, "Do you know what would be the consequences of your making this lion alive? Lion is a wild animal. It will kill all of us as soon as it gets life."

The third brother was adamant. He said, "My brothers have had the opportunity to show their skills. It is now my turn to show you that I can instill life in inanimate objects." Subuddhi protested, "Commonsense decrees that it is wise to keep away from criminals, lunatics, monsters, fire, swamp, angry and violent people. Their proximity is never beneficial." The third brother replied, "It is written in the *shastras* that even wild animals do not harm their benefactors. You will see that it would obey us."

Subuddhi got up and climbed a tree as he felt that he could not put any sense in his brother's head. The third brother put life in the lion. The lion got up and as it eyed the three brothers, pounced on them and made a meal of them. Then it sauntered into the forest. After some time Subuddhi climbed down and started for his home. He was extremely sorry for the death of his brothers who, in spite of being so learned, lacked ordinary commonsense. What could he do? He made all efforts to dissuade them but they themselves invited death by their foolish action. Those who do anything without thinking of the consequences, meet their end like them.

❏ ❏ ❏

10. A Terrified Demon

King Bhadrasen ruled over some city. His daughter Ratnavati was extraordinarily beautiful. A demon got enamoured of her and thought of abducting her from the palace. Her father had arranged for her safety through religious ceremonies and *tantrik* rituals. As such, the demon could not go near her. He made it a point to visit her bedroom. He remained invisible. Though the princess could not see him, yet she felt his presence as her entire body shivered at that time.

The princess felt miserable and as the situation became intolerable, she confided to a friend, "I am sick of this *vikral* demon. Please do something so that I can get rid of his evil presence." By coincidence, the demon was sitting in the corner of the room. As he heard the name of *vikral* demon, he thought that some demon of that name was also after the princess and the princess is scared of him. The princess had used the term 'vikral' to denote ferocious and actually she was talking about the demon in the room.

Anyway, the demon decided to find out about this *vikral* demon. He assumed the shape of a horse and hid in the stable. As he stood amongst the horses, a thief entered the stable to steal some horse. He cast his glance on all the horses to select the best amongst them. He chose the demon who stood amongst the horses in the shape of a fine horse.

The thief quickly put reins in the mouth of the demon and jumped on his back. The demon thought that he was the *vikral* demon about whom the princess was talking. He was convinced that *vikral* had come there to kill him. There were so many horses but only he was selected. He was helpless with the reins in his mouth and the thief astride him. The thief lashed him with a whip and he had no other option but to run for his life. The thief was terrified at the speed of the horse and thought of stopping it. He pulled at the reins but the horse increased its pace. Now the thief feared for his life. He tried all means to stop the horse but it was of no avail. The thief was convinced that he was riding some demon disguised as a horse. The demon meant to kill him. He looked around for some soft spot where he could jump off the back of the horse and save himself.

Soon he reached a banyan tree with overhanging branches that reached the ground. As the horse passed under the tree, he caught hold of a branch. While he swung in the air, the horse kept on running at a furious pace. A monkey, who was a friend of the demon, lived on that tree. The monkey recognised his friend in the guise of a horse and accosted him, "Why are you running away in fear of a mere mortal. This man is no demon but an ordinary thief. If you wish you can kill and eat him up." The demon stopped and came back to the tree.

The thief felt enraged at the intervention of the monkey. He could not harm it as it was sitting at a higher branch. He espied the monkey's tail dangling within reach. He started chewing the tail. The monkey in spite of being in great pain kept his cool. He could not let his demon friend feel that he was scared of the thief. The demon saw signs of pain on the face of the monkey and said, "You may say anything but I see signs of pain on your face. I think you are also under seize of the *vikral* demon. I am not going to stop here for another minute." So saying he ran away from the place.

❏ ❏ ❏

50 Wittiest Tales of BIRBAL

—Clifford Sawhney

Birbal's tales of wit and wisdom make lively reading for children as well as adults. His encounters at Emperor Akbar's Court are legendary.

Birbal's close friendship with Akbar earned him many enemies. Birbal survived countless murder attempts. Numerous stories have been spun around these plots. These stories were passed on from generation to generation. And the legend of Birbal grew. Unicorn Books presents 50 Birbal stories in this collection for children.

Pages: 120
Price: Rs. 48/- • Postage: Rs. 15/-

Tales of Wisdom

—Prof. A.P. Talwar

Moral-building 57 Tales for Children

Although education is meant to inculcate positive values in children to ensure a morally-sound future generation, thanks to economic compulsions, education is now solely geared towards competition and success. In today's chaotic environment, however, there is a dire need to impart the sound lessons of moral education to young impressionable minds.

Tales of Wisdom fills a significant void in this respect. Written chiefly for the younger generation (12-20 years) in simple and lucid language, it offers direct messages clothed in amusing and interesting tales. From how Ratnakar, a notorious dacoit, transformed into the great Maharshi Valmiki to how Swami Ram Teerth learnt the lesson of "the deeper the roots, the taller the tree", it offers innumerable pearls of wisdom designed to delight and teach at the same time.

The book is a must for personal, school and college libraries in order to ensure sound reading for children.

Demy Size • Pages: 136
Price: Rs. 72/- • Postage: Rs. 15/-

The Funniest Tales of Mullah Nasruddin

—Clifford Sawhney

The wittiest stories of the world's best-loved jester

Mullah Nasruddin is undoubtedly the best-known trickster and wit in human history. In some tales, Mullah is the smart joker taking others for a ride. In other stories, he's the one who becomes a fool. In yet others, the joke swings both ways and one isn't exactly sure who has fooled whom! Many tales are awash with unabashed nonsense and unbridled humour – where Nasruddin play the wise man, the fool, the victim or the prankster in turns!

For centuries, Nasruddin has been amusing people throughout the world. Indeed, Mullah's popularity was universally acknowledged when UNESCO declared 1996 as Nasruddin Hoja Year. His anecdotes are now being spun in modern avatars, with many tales of Mullah's exploits in America and England. This book deals with his tales of yore. After every tale, the author has added a creative insight. No matter what Mullah Nasruddin is called – a wise fool or a foolish wise man – there's no doubt he is the world's most loved trickster.

Pages: 144 • Price: Rs. 48/-
Postage: Rs. 15/-